ANOINTED
TO SING THE
GOSPEL

The Levitical Legacy of Thomas A. Dorsey

ANOINTED TO SING THE GOSPEL

The Levitical Legacy of Thomas A. Dorsey

KATHRYN B. KEMP

JOYFUL NOISE PRESS

Chicago

Praise for *Make a Joyful Noise: A Brief History of Gospel Music Ministry in America*

…The "Gospel section " of my CD collection includes: Yolanda Adams, Kirk Franklin, Donnie McClurkin, Fred Hammond, Mahalia Jackson, Sam Cooke, the Elvis Gospel Treasury, Aretha Franklin, and Ella Fitzgerald. That's it. Prior to reading Ms. Kemp's book, I had no knowledge of the gentlemen responsible for launching Gospel music into the mainstream of America: Thomas Dorsey and James Cleveland.
—Susan Delano, Wordpress.com

Make a Joyful Noise filled the three requirements for my reading satisfaction. Firstly, the extensive research gave me factual knowledge; then, the anecdotal episodes grounded those facts in living reality, and lastly, the love of her subject informed the whole book with—dare I say it—joy.
—Patricia Lambert, Writer

Dr. Kemp's book, *Make a Joyful Noise: A Brief History of Gospel Music Ministry in America,* was more than brief; it was loaded with all kinds of unusual gospel nuggets…This book is motivational, inspirational, and historical….
—Elder William R. Fuqua, Gospel Music Historian

Make a Joyful Noise by Kathryn Kemp is a gallant and gracious attempt to present a brief history of gospel music in America as a unique form of African American art. Ms. Kemp took great care in researching the many facets of gospel music, starting from its earliest beginning with the highly coded spiritual songs sung during slavery and the many contributors throughout the early twentieth century… *Make a Joyful Noise* is a mustread for all who want to know more about the genre of African American Gospel Music in America.
—Dr. Author Wright, Pastor and Theologian

Anointed to Sing the Gospel: The Levitical Legacy of Thomas A. Dorsey
© 2015 by Kathryn B. Kemp
Published by Joyful Noise Press, Chicago, Illinois

Queries regarding rights and permissions should be addressed to:
Joyful Noise Press, 8708 S. Bennett Ave., PMB 410, Chicago, IL 60617

Manufactured in the United States of America
Designed by: Sandra Williams

Publisher's Cataloging-In-Publication Data
(Prepared by The Donohue Group, Inc.)

Kemp, Kathryn B.
    Anointed to sing the Gospel : the Levitical legacy of Thomas A. Dorsey / by Kathryn B. Kemp.

     pages : illustrations, charts ; cm

    Issued also as an ebook.
    Includes bibliographical references and index.
    ISBN: 978-0-9833630-4-0

    1. Dorsey, Thomas Andrew. 2. Gospel musicians--United States--Biography. 3. African American composers--Biography. 4. Gospel music--United States--History and criticism. 5. National Convention of Gospel Choirs and Choruses, Inc. 6. Biography. I. Title.

ML410.D67 K46 2015
782.25/4092/0973

Dedication

This book is dedicated to the memory of my brother,
Roosevelt C. Baker, 1951-2015;

to Elder William R. Fuqua;
Pastor Nathan Schaffer, Jr.
Reverend Dr. Jeremiah A. Wright, Jr.;
and to all Levitical Families.

TABLE OF CONTENTS

About the Author

Kathryn Baker Kemp is a product of the Chicago Public Schools. She holds degrees from De Paul University (BA), Chicago State University (MS Ed), and Northern Illinois University (EdD). Her career as an educator encompassed duties as an elementary teacher, elementary counselor, high school dean, middle school assistant principal, and elementary school principal within CPS. She also taught as an adjunct faculty member for Northern Illinois University at the College of Du Page in Du Page County, Illinois.

Dr. Kemp's music ministry began with her first job as pianist for the Junior Choir of the Morning Star Baptist Church in Chicago. It ended in 2009 after 40 years of music ministry as organist, pianist, choir member, assistant choir director, minister of music, and director of music at Memorial M.B. Church in Chicago. Currently, she is active in the teaching ministry of her church, while serving as adjunct faculty at Chicago Baptist Institute International, teaching about African American music ministry. In April 2014, she became an ordained Baptist minister. She has been a member of the Chicago Metropolitan Allegro Mass Chapter of the Gospel Music Workshop of America since 2003 and a member of the national academic faculty of GMWA since 2007. She became a member of the National Convention of Gospel Choirs and Choruses in 2013.

The author works as a volunteer with civic and ministry groups and has also served on educational and financial advisory boards. Psalm 121, one of her favorite scriptures, guides her daily walk.

Foreword

Dr. Kathryn B. Kemp's two books on the ministry of gospel music highlight groundbreaking musicians and their contributions to black sacred and secular music. In her newest book, *Anointed to Sing the Gospel: The Levitical Legacy of Thomas A. Dorsey,* Kemp makes the case for "The Father of Gospel Music's" deserved recognition, not only as the preeminent gospel music composer, but also as a modern-day Levite.

Known by many names: "musician," "conductor," arranger," "poet," "prophet," and "shepherd," "Professor" Dorsey was the innovator and co-founder of The National Convention of Gospel Choirs and Choruses, the oldest black music convention in America. This convention has included the mission of keeping and preserving the composer's rich musical legacy in their heritage.

The writer of the foreword to this book was an avid collector of Dorsey's sheet music and books dating from the 1940s and 1950s and the guardian of the manuscripts which he so generously donated to the library of the Gospel Music Workshop of America.

In the beginning, music was ordained by God for a divine purpose, and that purpose was to worship and praise Him. Thus, music became the most important language known to mankind. Indeed, it is the mode of communication that speaks to our total emotions, spirit, will, mind, and body. By keeping Dorsey's music alive, we are preserving a priceless cultural legacy of creative works that embody lyrics which spoke eloquently to social movements in our country and the world in powerful words of prayer and praise. Examples of these songs include: "I Know the Lord Will Make a Way, Oh! Yes He Will;" "I'm Going to Live the Life I Sing About in My Song;" and his signature composition, "Precious Lord, Take My Hand."

"The Levitical generation, theologically stated in the Bible, began with the birth of Jacob and Leah's third son, Levi, in Genesis 29:34. The Levites were musicians who also performed several other jobs in the Temple, as described in 2 Chronicles 5:12. A careful reading of the fifth chapter of the second book of Chronicles provides the reader of this book with valuable insight about this priestly class as a frame of reference for understanding the Levitical aspect of the life of Thomas A. Dorsey.

Through her research, travels, and interviews, Dr. Kemp, both in this book, and her earlier book, *Make a Joyful Noise: A Brief History of Gospel Music Ministry in America*, has compiled a record of our sacred musical heritage that dates from pre-slavery to the twenty-first century. This recorded history is the "true foundation," "our plumb line," that keeps the structure of our musical legacy on a straight and firm footing.

Kemp's 2011 book, *Make a Joyful Noise: A Brief History of Gospel Music Ministry in America,* was anything but brief: it was chock full of details and little known facts about a musical idiom that historians have long neglected as a uniquely African American art form.

This book, *Anointed to Sing the Gospel: The Levitical Legacy of Thomas A. Dorsey,* by focusing on the one individual who is most responsible for the creation of the "gospel song," is a welcome and worthy addition to the field of gospel music ministry. It makes for the perfect companion to Kemp's earlier book for those who want to better understand the origin and development of contemporary gospel music in America.

Elder William R. Fuqua, M.Div
Gospel Historian

Acknowledgments

"I can do all things through Christ
who strengthens me."
Philippians 4:13

There are many who shared insights, revelations, and knowledge with the author in this endeavor. All contributions have enriched and informed my writing. I am grateful to those who consented to have their interviews included for this work and to those who provided pictures and personal stories about Thomas A. Dorsey.

Special thanks to the colleges and universities who shared their archives: Chicago Public Library, Carter G. Woodson Branch, Vivian G. Harsh Research Collection, Harsh Research Librarians; Columbia College Center for Black Music Research, Chicago, Janet Harper, Librarian; and the Fisk University, John Franklin Hope Library, Thomas A. Dorsey Archives, Aisha Johnson, Special Collections Librarian.

Thanks are extended to Ebenezer Missionary Baptist Church - Chicago, Illinois and Mt. Prospect Baptist Church, Villa Rica, Georgia. I also wish to thank Deb Wise of the Ma Rainey Museum, Columbus, Georgia.

Kudos are extended to my editor, Mark Boone for crafting this work into the finished product. Finally, with heartfelt gratitude, I wish to thank all who provided original artifacts, as well as mentors, friends and family who have challenged, and encouraged me as I worked to share the rich legacy of our music and our story.

Introduction

The importance of African American sacred music, the African American religious experience, and twenty-first century gospel music and worship are the ties that bind this work. The music, created by our African ancestors, is the seam of the African American religious heritage. Therefore, it must be honored and preserved for future generations at all costs. Music, whether sacred or secular, is a universal language. It connects with the emotions of a people. It is part of life and death. Music invokes happiness and sorrow, victory and defeat, worship and sensuality. It exists in all societies and rites, both sacred and profane.

There has never been a separation of the sacred and the secular music in the lifestyle of African people. Music was, and is, a part of the rhythm—the heartbeat of life. This holistic view of life emanated from the African belief system and values. Life, viewed holistically, can be seen through two lenses: objectively and subjectively. Rational-articulate, intuitive-knowing are part of the African world view. This author uses this multidimensional mode of seeing—the use of different but equally important knowledge systems—as a construct to define values, beliefs, and behavior as illustrated in the author's Knowledge Construct (See Appendix II).

Europeans viewed music differently from Africans. European music of the Catholic, Lutheran, and Anglican churches was marked by plainsong, chants, hymns, and anthems based on a seven-note diatonic scale. African music, on the other hand, used instruments and bodily rhythmic patterns and was based on the five-note pentatonic scale. The music Africans heard in church services after they were brought to America during the Middle Passage was very different from the music of their homeland. African slaves invented their own musical style—"folk music"—that was the genesis of all musical genres in America.

Thomas Andrew Dorsey dared to bring the secular and sacred together in the early twentieth century. He coined the phrase "gospel song" to describe his original compositions. While gospel hymns were not new to the body of African American sacred music, Dorsey is credited with fusing a secular rhythm with sacred music and its lyrics, and, in so doing, with revolution-izing church worship for mainline African American churches.

The purpose of this book is threefold. It is to chronicle the life of Thomas A. Dorsey and his contributions to music—both sacred and secular. It is to explore his life in Georgia and in Chicago, Illinois. It is to examine his legacy as the acknowledged "Father of Gospel Music" from the perspectives of a shepherd, a prophet, and a "Levitical priest."

In her 1935 biography *The Life and Works of Thomas Andrew Dorsey*, Ruth Smith characterizes the musical trailblazer and genius as a shep-herd/poet. That analogy was based on the similar qualities she saw in his leadership when compared to those of the shepherd who became king—David. Not only was David a shepherd, but he was also a poet who poured his heart out to God in Psalms, which he composed as songs for his people to sing in worship to God. David, more than any other bibli-cal character, combined several unique gifts he possessed as a leader. He wrote for the Levites who were in charge of the sanctuary and the temple; he designed the leadership structure for praise and worship in the temple; he assigned duties for its singers and dancers; he assigned duties to those charged with the care of the temple and of its contents. Moreover, he fought his enemies to achieve the gains that he believed were necessary for his people. The prophetic aspect of his nature is established by his many lyrical compositions that address a personal relationship with God and the righteousness necessary to inherit the Kingdom of Heaven. These prophetic lessons are shared through his songs, poems, and teaching.

Prophecy is defined in First Corinthians 14 as that which is edi-fying to the people of God. In that vein, Dorsey's songbooks were titled *Songs with a Message* and *Songs for the Kingdom*. During his workshops, he frequently provided brief synopses of the meanings of his songs and per-formances. These songbooks were developed for the exclusive use of the National Convention of Gospel Choirs and Choruses, the musical organi-zation he co-founded and the oldest Black music convention in America. These songs gave comfort and reassurance to people who were hearing and singing the good news of the gospel during bad times.

Dorsey's legacy as a shepherd shares similarities with the priestly legacy of the Old Testament Levites when seen through the lens of the National Convention of Gospel Choirs and Choruses. The convention is dedicated not only to preserving his music and legacy, but to training youth for service in church music and as worship leaders, much as the rules and laws embodied in the Old Testament Book of Leviticus did for the priestly class and those assigned to them.

Make A Joyful Noise: A Brief History of Gospel Music Ministry in America (Kemp, 2011) touched on aspects of this legacy, one which is still disputed to this day. This book seeks to portray the fullness of Dorsey's contributions to music, both sacred and secular, through the prophetic gift, the shepherding spirit, and the Levitical legacy, while addressing the function of the gospel song in twentieth and twenty-first century America.

Thomas Dorsey invented a style of singing for soloists: most often modeled by Sallie Martin and Mahalia Jackson. These two women frequently performed his compositions at conventions and programs to demonstrate the style and feeling that each song was intended to communicate to its listener. Sallie Martin, for her part, toured the country organizing unions for the convention and demonstrating the vocal techniques that she had learned from Dorsey.

Several of his compositions, labeled eponymously as "a Dorsey," were dedicated to specific singers—members of his fold—or "Dorsey disciples." Because of his contribution to the gospel music genre of the 1940s, most gospel music was identified with the eponym "Dorsey's."

The legacies of both of his sacred and secular contributions to music are celebrated annually in his hometown of Villa Rica, Georgia. In June 2014, the twentieth annual Thomas A. Dorsey Fest culminated with a three-day event that began the last weekend of the month. The official program cover, designed by co-chairperson and Birthplace Choir Director Eric Ayers, blended the many faces of Thomas A. Dorsey throughout the years. The festival is one of three annual events sponsored by the town of Villa Rica and other supporters.

Dorsey's legacy as a shepherd continues in the music of twenty-first century gospel singers who continually improvise and refine the musical riffs and chords that produce the genre that we know today as "contemporary gospel." The irony is that many of these young musicians have no idea of whom to thank for the very foundation through which their gifts and talents are displayed. Few, if any know that the gospel "special chorus" was invented by Thomas A. Dorsey.

The history of black religious music is rich and diverse. Music is inherent in the personal life, psyche, and community life of people of African ancestry. It is a part of every ritual and tradition that gives meaning and purpose to how we define our worth. It was born in crisis, when blacks were counted as three-fifths of a person. Music—sacred and secular—was a sustaining force in the life of our ancestors. It has addressed civil rights issues in America as well as injustice throughout the world. It is a powerful tool which helps to shape and define the cultural landscape of our reality.

It is hoped that a reexamination of the legacy of Thomas A. Dorsey can serve as a touchstone for the sacred artists and musicians of the twenty-first century and beyond. Their music, too, can positively shape, define, address, and transform this society. A theology of liberation is as much needed in the twenty-first century of "Stand Your Ground" laws and spiritual blindness as it was during the Jewish Exodus, The Civil War, Post Reconstruction, and Jim Crow atrocities. New freedom songs reminiscent of those that fueled the Civil Rights Era are needed. Contemporary messages from African-American music, whether sacred or secular, are desperately needed to mobilize and energize this present age to address the racial and economic disparities of our era. African Americans indeed matter during this century, as in others, to God.

Chapter One

Early Influences on Thomas Dorsey's Musical Career

Thomas Andrew Dorsey was born at the turn of the nineteenth century in Villa Rica, Georgia, 37 miles west of Atlanta on July 1, 1899. The eldest of five children of Thomas Madison Dorsey and Etta (nee) Plant, he had two brothers: Lloyd and Curtis, and two sisters: Lovie and Bernice. Thomas Dorsey senior was born circa 1857, and Etta Plant Dorsey, circa 1873. The elder Dorsey was a member of the first generation to obtain higher education post slavery, having graduated with a Bachelor of Divinity degree from Atlanta Baptist College, later to become Morehouse University. An itinerant preacher, he never pastored a church (Reagon, 2001, 68-69).

Both mother and father were scions of respected families in the town of Villa Rica. Etta Plant Dorsey was a church organist and pianist from a musically gifted family who had been widowed when her first husband died in a railroad car accident. A preacher and part-time teacher, Thomas Dorsey Sr. was known for his flamboyant style of preaching, frequently using props as aids both to embellish and drive home the themes of his sermons. Such theatrics impressed his young namesake, who reminisces about his earliest exposure to such music in an interview with Steve Turner:

> My mother was an organist in one of the country
> churches when I was a little fellow, and my father was
> an itinerant preacher travelling from place to place,

and sometimes he'd take me along as company. In
that way, I got my experience; quite a bit of it for music, quite a bit of it for travel, quite a bit of it for liking
to meet people (Turner, 2010, 62).

The younger Dorsey soon began imitating his father's style of preaching, going under the porch of the family house to deliver his "sermons," using a cane similar to that of his father's.

Etta Dorsey had received her musical training while vacation-
ing in New York and Chicago with her first husband. He, a railroad
employee, had died while trying to board a railcar. The portable organ that Etta Dorsey played was carried between each location of her
husband's church services (McLin Interview, 2014). Young Thomas
Dorsey found the models for his early secular musical pursuits in the
lives of his mother's brother and brother-in-law. He gravitated to one
of them, his maternal uncle, Phil Plant, a famous blues guitarist who
lived in the area.

Early Life in Villa Rica, Georgia

Life in Villa Rica was privileged in many ways for young Dorsey. His
family was well-known and respected, worshipping at the Mt. Prospect Baptist Church in Villa Rica from time to time. Corrie Hinds-
man, an uncle of Thomas's, was a teacher in the Villa Rica school
system. He introduced blacks at Mt. Prospect Baptist Church to
"shape-note singing," a style of singing that began in New England
in Puritan churches during the early 1700s. By 1815, the style had
become a means of teaching reading to black children in the South.
The textbook, *The Sacred Harp*, addressed shape-note singing and
was instrumental in giving former slaves who had not been educated
an avenue by which to become literate. Teacher Ananias Davisson is

credited with developing this method of singing to which Dorsey was introduced at an early age. (Reagon, 2001, 167).

Thomas learned many lessons on the family's front porch at night, the customary gathering place during the Georgia summer evenings where neighbors and relatives would often stop. He heard sounds that can best be described as moaning, an important element in the development of Black sacred music, though, at the time he didn't understand how those moanings could lead to shouts. Later, they were absorbed into Thomas Dorsey's DNA to inform the music and heritage of a new African-American music art form—the gospel song.

Walker (1987) identifies a genre of African American folk music common in the rural South, termed "hymns of improvisation." These hymns were part of the prayer and praise tradition of the southern church. They sprung from the stories shared by blacks' over night fires and family porches. Booker T. Washington called them "spirits that dwell in deep woods" (Walker, 1991, xvi).

Dorsey also learned many lessons about love and Christian charity from his mother, an intensely religious woman who held daily family worship with Bible readings and devotion. Kind to everyone, Etta Plant Dorsey made a point of performing acts of kindness, biblically called "the spiritual gift of mercy." She fed hobos and other strangers. Dorsey called her a woman with "unquenchable faith" (*Inspirational Thoughts, 59*).

Employment was difficult to come by in the small town of Villa Rica. Setbacks in 1903 led to a reversal in the family's fortunes. Etta Plant Dorsey had inherited land that she was forced to mortgage and that was eventually lost for unpaid taxes. Michael Harris, Dorsey's biographer, states that "even though figures in the county land and tax records show that the actual aggregate value of the land increased between 1903 and 1907, the elder Dorsey was forced to become a sharecropper for a white farmer," a role that was insufficient to meet the family's economic needs. It also was a source of dishonor for this proud and educated black man (Reagon, 169).

The Move to Atlanta

The inability to earn a sustainable living forced the family's move to Atlanta in 1908. The loss of prestige in the city of Atlanta was coupled with economic disappointment. Dorsey's father found work as a porter or laborer according to the Atlanta City Directory published during the years 1909 to 1915. Etta, for the first time in her married life, was forced to take in washing to supplement the family income (U.S. Census 1910). She is listed as a laundress in the Atlanta City Directory. These changes also led to a deterioration in her overall health, contributing to her suffering from bouts of illness during Thomas's boyhood years (Reagon, 1992, 170-173).

Conditions worsened for young Dorsey when he encountered Atlanta's unspoken black "class system." He suddenly went from the status of a privileged preacher's son to that of a country bumpkin. Demoted a year in school, his classmates made fun of him, ridiculing him for his clothes and speech. To deepen his sense of isolation, he was excluded from their parties, a rejection that caused him to drop out of school at about the age of ten.

Dorsey's Changing Fortunes

Dorsey's fortunes began to turn when he started taking piano lessons from Mrs. Graves, a teacher who operated a music studio near Morehouse College with which she was affiliated. She was the only music teacher who taught the black folk at that time (Broughton, 1985, 33). This necessitated Dorsey's travelling by foot to the upper middle class section of town. He walked more than thirty miles a week to and from

Graves's house, Dorsey recalled. There, he learned technique and fingering, a marked advancement from the rote playing he had learned in the past. Moreover, he enrolled at Morehouse College and took a class on harmony. Having decided that he had learned enough from Graves, he left her tutelage to learn how to play the piano for the movies that had become a staple of entertainment during that period.

Dorsey displayed an entrepreneurial bent at a young age. He knew how to earn money by working in the circus carrying water and doing other errands. He played for Saturday night dances—sometimes with pay—before he became a teenager (Broughton, 33). His first job working in the theatre was selling drinks and popcorn for five cents to the entertainers during intermission at the 81 Theatre on Auburn Avenue in Atlanta. The theater was a vaudeville house located on Decatur Street (Boyer 1995, 58). Auburn Avenue and Decatur Street intersected in Atlanta's dangerous black night life district. Stabbings and murders were common on weekends. This was the place where one could find music, booze, and women at the barrelhouses that populated the district. Barrelhouses were also called "juke joints," where the music played had a two-beat rhythm and was frequently called "honky-tonk" and "boogie-woogie." One could also find dance clubs, theatres, and restaurants in this section of Atlanta (Muwakkil, *The Reader* 1978, Sec. 1, 28).

This was the entertainment that both captivated and fascinated young Dorsey. The 81 Theater was a principal booking agency for The Theater Owners Booking Association—the same association that later booked shows for Dorsey and his contemporary, the noted blues singer of the day, "Ma" Rainey. This theatre booked all the top black entertainers on the circuit (Boyer, 58). The streets were run by three black gangsters named "Handsome Harry, Lucky Sambo, and Joe Slocum." Dorsey recalls the early years of his musical development: (Broughton, 33).

As a boy I sold pop, ginger ale, and red rock at the 81 Theater, and I got a chance to meet all the stars, all the performers that came to the theatre to play. And there they'd want a pop or something, a cold drink on credit until payday, and I got a chance to know them all! I stayed 'round that theatre; I'd hang around the theatre, and I learned a lot. And I learned blues; I could play piano, and I think it paid off very well for me (Broughton, 33).

Dorsey Hears Gertrude "Ma" Rainey Sing

Dorsey learned a few songs from Ed Butler, the pianist at the 81 for whom he sometimes would fill in, but he lacked steady work. A precocious child, Dorsey was only ten years old at the time, and he kept the job for two years. It was there that he first heard Ma Rainey sing.

He was fascinated with the blues, paying close attention to the chords and rhythms of the barrelhouse piano. Dorsey, as part of his early musical training, frequented theaters and dance halls, listening to the musicians and learning what he could from them. He also started to make his rounds to the "house parties," travelling with the "local luminaries Lark Lee, 'Long Boy,' Nome Burke, and James Henningway" and earning the nickname "Barrelhouse Tom." (Yazoo, 1041, 3). Such contact with musicians developed in him the characteristics that he was able to incorporate into his own unique musical style. Dorsey, during this period continued to play by day for churches in Atlanta while learning blues chords and riffs in the city's nightclubs by night.

These early musical influences would become apparent through both the secular and sacred music that Dorsey composed throughout his lifetime. He later became known as a barrelhouse pianist while he earned money in Chicago as "Georgia Tom," the nickname given to him by Mayo "Ink" Williams, the recording director of Paramount Studio in 1928. Dorsey used this pseudonym to record many albums. Such influences also formed the basis for the gospel songs he would compose, songs infused with a barrelhouse style that met with ire from the Baptist pastors in Chicago. "It wasn't proper church music," they huffily remarked.

Dorsey, as a child prodigy, had mastered many instruments, but he now added blues and ragtime to his repertoire of spirituals and church music (Muwakkil, 28). Thus, he was able to master all genres of black music before becoming an adult. Using the money that he earned in Atlanta playing the piano at bordellos, house rent parties, and women's teas, he was able to supplement the family's income. Eventually, he saved enough money to leave Atlanta for good and to journey to the North to follow his dream to pursue his musical talents and a career as a professional musician. His first stop was in Philadelphia, Pennsylvania circa 1915.

The Chicago "Rent Party" Circuit

The Chicago Dorsey saw was only slightly different from the city that other southern migrants saw in 1916, yet he saw more opportunities in Chicago than existed in other major northern cities: "I migrated to Chicago, where I had the opportunity to become a great musician" (Kalil: Dorsey, Interview, 1961, 79-80). He chose Chicago because he was impressed with its musical possibilities.

Although Dorsey had established a name for himself throughout Atlanta's "house rent party circuit" during the years 1911 to 1916, he found, however, after his arrival in the North in 1916, that work was not as plentiful for musicians as he had imagined, a fact that was exacerbated by his lack of a union card. Horace Boyer asserts that

Dorsey first moved to Gary, Indiana, in 1916, where he found employment at the steel mills, and later relocated to Chicago in 1918 (Boyer, 2000, 58).

It was in Chicago that he quickly established his own "house rent party circuit." Dorsey muses about those early Chicago days in the PBS Documentary, "We've Come This Far by Faith, Pt. 3."

> When the immigrants began to come in—I am talking about from the South now—they'd have to raise this rent money, and they would have what they called house rent parties to raise their money. And I got in with a bunch there, and I had a house rent party to play every night (PBS Documentary, "We've Come This Far by Faith," 4).

Having previously established a reputation as a blues and house party player in Atlanta, Dorsey found that he nevertheless had to begin over again in Chicago, owing largely to the fact that he lacked the necessary music credentials required by Chicago union professionals. Musicians in Chicago had established standards for pay scales, restrictions that affected not only their availability to obtain work, but also the amount they could charge for their musical talents. He moved swiftly to resolve this problem. He knew that he had to secure the needed credentials to earn top dollar and to fulfill his goals. He set out therefore, to get the qualifications needed to meet the city's music union criteria. He worked during the day and attended the Chicago College of Composition and Arranging from 1918 to 1919 at night to study music (Smith, 1935).

He had to work multiple jobs to survive. Thus, in 1918, shortly after settling in Chicago, he began to perform with local jazz groups, one of which was the "Whispering Serenaders," which, at one time, featured Lionel Hampton. He also found employment with a five-piece jazz orchestra while continuing to work at the U.S. Steel Mill in Gary and attending night school (Boyer, 58).

Dorsey's Second Conversion

In Dorsey's words, God spoke to him in the midst of his quest for secular fame. Although he had accepted Christ as a child growing up in Georgia, a second conversion through the power of the Holy Spirit occurred for him in 1921. He received an epiphany after attending the annual service of the National Baptist Convention that met in Chicago that year. It was then that he experienced, first-hand, the power of "sacred gospel music." He relived the experience in an interview with Steve Turner:

> There was a Baptist convention up the street from where I was staying. I was playing rags and blues at parties and things on Saturday nights. There was a fellow who came to the convention by the name of Nix who stayed with my uncle, and he got up one night and sang "I Know a Great Savior, I Do Don't You?" After he'd finished, the minister said that anyone could join the church. If you were interested, they would send you to a church of your choice. I thought, "Here's my chance." I was playing jazz music. In fact, I was working in clubs. So I quit. I walked off my job (Turner, 62).

Dorsey then became a pianist at a small Baptist church, New Hope, on the south side of Chicago. The conversion was short-lived: the meager salary wasn't enough to pay his bills, so he continued to play in jazz clubs.

The Rise in Popularity of "Race Records"

In the early 1920s, the recording industry in the United States saw a market in what was termed "race records." Among its purveyors was Paramount Studio, whose strategies were devised solely to sell products to black people. Evangelists and singing preachers were included in this marketing strategy. These recording companies dangled the carrot of jobs and fame to the migrating blues musicians. This enticement increased the economic possibilities of entertainers and musicians like Dorsey who were emerging onto Chicago's expanding musical scene.

At this time, the popularity of the blues was increasing, both in New York and Chicago, and especially among non-black audiences. Chicago quickly became known as the blues capital of the urban North. By 1924, Dorsey was playing with the "Whispering Syncopators," an experience that led to his touring in theaters and dance halls. Dorsey now also became eligible for membership in the Musicians' Protective Union and was paid their standard wages for his work. Finally, he had reached the level of distinction he had sought, earning a salary equal to that of professional theater musicians (Drake, 1940, 171).

Chicago as a Blues Magnet. Chicago's secular music scene was also a magnet for other musicians from the South who chose to make Chicago their home, bypassing New York, a trend that had begun as early as 1902, when New Orleans musicians began migrating to Chicago. "Jelly Roll" Morton, Joe "King" Oliver and Louis Armstrong were among the first to arrive in Chicago. "Tampa Red," "Little Brother" Montgomery, "Blind John" Davis, "Blind Lemon" Jefferson, and Dorsey became other well-known secular entertainers who chose Chicago over Harlem (Kalil 1983, 82-83). This was fulfillment of what Dorsey expected from the city that would make him famous. James

10

Arnold (Georgia), Charles Davenport (Alabama), "Sonny Boy" Williamson (Tennessee), and "Muddy Waters" (Mississippi) also gravitated to the city because of Chicago's prominence in jazz and blues. All were viewed as profit streams for Paramount, notwithstanding the fact that the promises made to them were not always lived up to (Kalil, 1993, 84).

Chicago's South Side: An Entertainment Mecca. Black life in this imposed enclave of Chicago's South Side was rich in culture. The south side entertainment area known as the "Levee District," developed in Chicago's black community. It was located from South State Street to the Chicago River between Polk and 16th Streets. It later moved to 22nd and State Streets and became known as the "Tenderloin District." This spread of blacks into other areas of the city expanded the boundaries of the black community.   New entertainment districts eventually would flourish within these expanded boundaries.

"Blues music," Bruck asserts, could be heard throughout the community in what became known as "Black and Tan Clubs," white-owned jazz clubs that were patronized by whites on weekends but were integrated on weekdays. The area best known for these clubs was nicknamed "The Stroll," located at 35th and State Streets.

After 1920, this area became the center of black entertainment. Its boundaries expanded as blacks moved further south, stretching the limits to 47th Street once the Savoy Ballroom and Regal Theaters were built. Nicknamed "Black Broadway," the area further expanded the Black community that in the first decade of the twentieth century had been dubbed by social scientists as "The Black Metropolis." It continued to draw several artists and writers to the community. (For an in-depth discussion of the development of this cultural enclave, the social conditions that spawned its emergence, and Thomas A. Dorsey's inspiration to write gospel songs as a way of proclaiming the

"Good News in bad times," see Appendix I: "Emerging Black Culture: 1890-1930.)

Dorsey, ever the versatile musician, was able to effortlessly adapt his musical style to the tastes of the day, unlike blues singers such as Bessie Smith, who preferred to adhere to the traditional southern idiom still popular among black Americans. While Dorsey had played occasionally for Bessie Smith, it was Gertrude Pridgett, better known as "Ma Rainey," who was the secular blues artist most closely associated with his early blues career.

While Dorsey honed his skills in the secular music industry making a name for himself, he continued his pursuits in the field of sacred music, printing and selling sacred sheet music in 1925 for the composer and director Charles Pace. Pace and his Pace Jubilee Singers were denied royalties by their label Victor Phonograph, who used the excuse that their music had not been printed or copyrighted. They appealed to Dorsey to write their music and print it for them. Dorsey, understanding the politics of "race records," willingly agreed. He was well aware of the profits the record companies made from the evangelical singing sermons, black quartets, and jubilee music. He had deployed the skills he developed at the Chicago College of Composition and Arranging to get a job with Paramount Studio's music publishing arm, where he began working in 1923. While there, he wrote "lead sheets for $3.00 a piece of recorded music for copyright purposes (Drake, 173)."

Unscrupulous Record Promoters. It was at Paramount that Dorsey discovered that the record companies cheated the performers out of their full royalties because they didn't own the title to their music. Paramount, for its part, used an African American, Mayo "Ink" Williams, to procure black talent for them, and he became the unofficial "director" of Paramount's black race records division. Williams, ultimately realizing his need to recoup some of the profit he was losing from these dealings, started his own company, The Chicago Music Publishing Company, and hired Dorsey to work for him.

Ironically, both men robbed other black artists from the full amount due them for their work, a fate that had befallen Dorsey himself, as he, too, was forced to relinquish the copyright to some of his own songs. Dorsey, therefore, inexplicably became a part of a system that denied singers their copyrights, just as he had been cheated in the past.

Promoters would bring artists to the Chicago Music Publishing Company. The artists would sing a few lines. Dorsey would complete the musical score, but would not give the artist credit for the lyrics. This appears to have been common practice in the early years of gospel recording (Drake, 171-175).

Dorsey's Association with Ma Rainey

Dorsey also shared his own compositions with some of Paramount's star attractions, vaudeville singers who included Ma Rainey and Trixie Smith. He composed more than two hundred blues songs between 1923 and 1932, some of them early compositions sung by Rainey (Yazoo, 1041, 3). He also wrote original compositions for Ma Rainey. Rainey, the possessor of a throbbing contralto voice, had talent and appeal that convinced Paramount to market her songs, and notably, she also became the first woman to have her picture on a Paramount record album (Wise Interview, 2013).

Gertrude "Ma" Rainey, born in Columbus, Georgia on April 26, 1886, personified the new generation of blues singers. She began performing as a girl of twelve or fourteen years of age. She married Will "Pa" Rainey in 1904 and toured the South with him as part of F.S. Wolcott's Rabbit Foot Minstrels. The couple later formed their own group, which they named Rainey and Rainey Assassinators of the Blues. Ma Rainey has been billed as "The Mother of the Blues," having recorded more than one hundred records in the mid-1920s. Dorsey became her bandleader and arranger, having first seen her as a boy while working the theatres of Atlanta.

Dorsey Adopts the Name "Georgia Tom." Dorsey was re-introduced to Ma Rainey in Chicago by Mayo Williams. It was also there that Dorsey adopted the moniker "Georgia Tom." He performed with her band and with his own jazz band "Texas Tommy and Friends" into the early 1930s. His first blues composition was "A Good Man is Hard to Find" (Mt. Prospect Baptist Church Archives). Ma Rainey and her Wild Cats Jazz Band led by Thomas Dorsey debuted at the Grand Theater in Chicago in 1924. They toured with the Theater Owner Booking Association in the southern and midwestern states from 1924 to 1926. During this time he met and married Nettie Harper in 1925. She became Ma Rainey's wardrobe coordinator and dresser. She was in charge of the costumes and props for the shows.

Dorsey didn't work with Ma Rainey again until 1928. Some speculate that the reason for the lull was a nervous breakdown that Dorsey suffered. His niece believes, however, that it was the result of the "Holy Spirit dealing with him." (McLin Interview, 2014.)

In an article in *The Reader*, "The Father of Gospel Music," Dorsey gave a detailed account of life with Ma Rainey. Says Dorsey: "She was in a class by herself. No one could do what she did...amazing performer... but it was her personality that really made her popular." (Muwakkil, 28).

He went on to recall an incident that influenced his decision to leave what he termed "theater life" to "work for the Lord." Unknowingly, Ma Rainey had bought stolen jewelry when they were performing in Cleveland at the Bijou Theater, and two detectives came backstage to detain her. She was arrested with the money to pay the band in her possession. The group was left with no money and another show scheduled in a nearby town. Her entourage attempted to pass a member of the troupe off as Ma Rainey, but the ploy failed. The show was closed on the spot. Dorsey got back to Chicago as soon as he could.

Dorsey Decides to Leave Theater Life. As a result of the experience, Dorsey began evaluating the lifestyle he was living. Ma Rainey returned three days later, with the issue resolved. She was ready to go back on the road, but Dorsey chose not to go with her. He states: "But by then I had decided to give up theater life and dedicate myself to the Lord, so I said no. That was it. I've never returned to that life, and I have no regrets about my decision." (Muwakkil, "The Father of Gospel," 30).

A second incident associated with Dorsey's decision to leave the theater life is speculated to have occurred in 1926 and to account for the two years that he didn't appear with Ma Rainey. Dorsey, at a performance one night for her, lost his equilibrium and felt the room spin. It was unclear at the time whether it was due to stage fright or something else. Subsequently, he went through a period of depression and was unable to work for two years (Turner, 59). Harris includes this account in a transcription for the PBS Documentary, "We've Come This Far by Faith, Part 3," to describe Dorsey's experience.

> He said that he is playing at this club, and he tries to play some more and he can't. I would say to him, what happened? Were you paralyzed, a numbness? He doesn't remember any of these things, and he said, but I know my fingers—I know I could move my fingers. I just couldn't play. Think of that. I have the muscular ability to move, but I can't play. In other words, I can't make music. I can't create (PBS Documentary, "We've Come This Far by Faith,"7).

Ma Rainey's Decline. Ma Rainey's career declined in the 1930s because of the Great Depression and a change in economic conditions. She retired completely from performing in 1935 and returned to her native Georgia, where she cared for family members until their death. She died on December 22, 1939 in Rome, Georgia. Her brother, a church official, refused to honor her musical legacy on her death certificate, listing her occupation as a housekeeper (Wise Interview).

Rainey's museum, which is located in her hometown of Columbus, Georgia, is funded by the city, and it sits on the land that was once her home. It houses a history of her career and many artifacts, albums, and photographs that chronicled her career. Deb Wise, a docent hired by the city of Columbus, conducts tours. She met with the author in October 2013 and shared Ma Rainey's colorful history and legacy (Wise Interview).

The museum is replete with photographs, vinyl record covers, and albums. Memorabilia in the form of letters and awards cover the walls. Blues and jazz artists associated with Ma Rainey include Bessie Smith, Mamie Smith, Louis Armstrong, and the Georgia Jazz Band. A commemorative 29-cent postage stamp was issued in 1994 by the U.S. Postal Office in her honor. Her song "See See Rider Blues" (1925) was inducted into the Grammy Hall of Fame (Rainey Museum).

Dorsey's Secular Music Success

Thomas Dorsey, by now established both in sacred and secular music composition, continued to perform with other musicians as well as with his own band. He again performed with Ma Rainey and with his own jazz band "Texas Tommy and Friends" into the early 1930s. Those performers included Bobby Robinson; Aletha Dickerson, a piano player; and Tommy Ladnier (Yazoo, 1041, 5). Dorsey is thought to have used blues guitarists more than other blues pianists of the 1920s.

This may in part have stemmed from his childhood love for the blues played by his uncle Phil Plant.

Dorsey's first blues composition "A Good Man is Hard to Find" is noted in the records of his birthplace church (Mt. Prospect Baptist Church Archives). Although Dorsey first began writing music in 1921, the credit for his secular music success and fame cannot be attributed to his association with Ma Rainey alone. He worked with blues guitarists who included "Scrapper Blackwell," Leroy Carr, and "Big Bill" Bronzy in the studio, as well as with Kansas City vocalist Frankie "Half-Pint" Jason and Mozelle Ardson ("Kansas City Kitty"), Hannah May, and Jane Lucas in the recording studio (Yazoo 1041, 6). His versatility can be seen yet again in the 1920s urban style of blues called "Hokum," the name given to a new sound that was prevalent during the Roaring Twenties (Humphrey, 4). It became the title for the earliest form of city blues that featured double entendres and lyrics considered to be "disreputable, shallow, and artless" (Yazoo, 1041, 2).

Dorsey Teams Up with "Tampa Red." Dorsey, also known as "Georgia Tom," and Hudson Woodbridge, known only as "Tampa Red" became the "the Hokum Boys," a nickname adopted at the suggestion of Aletha Dickerson and Bobby Robinson, arrangers for a record company. (Yazoo, 1041). Paradoxically, Dorsey was also credited with raising "blues music to new levels of inventiveness" and bringing a "degree of wit and sophistication that had never previously been known to blues lyrics," an assessment that is antithetical to the definition of "hokum" (Yazoo, 2).

Black singers performed under multiple labels to increase their revenue streams. Dorsey was no different than other artists. He recorded with two separate groups while he wrote for other blues artists. His earnings from secular music were more than enough to cover family expenses. "Maybe It's the Blues," "Last Minute Blues," (used by

Ma Rainey on her debut session), and "Grieving Blues," a song Dorsey used on his own solo recording debut, were listed as some of his all-time favorites (Yazoo, 2).

"It's Tight Like That." "Tampa Red" is the blues guitarist most closely associated with "Georgia Tom's" fame. He met Dorsey in 1925 when he came to Chicago. He came to Dorsey and showed him the lyrics to the song "It's Tight Like That," asking Dorsey to compose the musical arrangement. The two made their recording debut with the song in 1928 on the record label Vocation. The song brought them instantaneous fame. This was seven years after Dorsey's second conversion experience in 1921. During the time, Dorsey was also the musician for the New Hope Baptist Church. It is documented that Dorsey refused Tampa's entreaties to work with him for three hours before finally consenting to write the music for his lyrics. They recorded the piece the following day. The record company knew it would become a big hit. The song was also recorded with different lyrics, lyrics which almost resulted in its banning (Yazoo, 1014, 4).

"It's Tight Like That" was also recorded for OKeh records. The duo also recorded other songs using different names. This greatly increased their personal revenues. According to Dorsey, his association with Tampa Red "paid off in a great way" (Yazoo, 1041, 4). "It's Tight Like That" was the most imitated blues song of the 1920s. It contained nothing that would suggest the Levitical heritage or destiny of the man known as Georgia Tom.

W.C. Handy dubbed "It's Tight Like That" the forerunner of the "lowdown dirty blues" (Yazoo, 1041, 4). The *Chicago Defender* newspaper, the city's eminent black newspaper in the November 23, 1929 issue remarked that:

> "Everybody has heard "It's Tight Like That," and everybody has danced to it....And lately a symphonic

arrangement of the naughty blues number has been made by Mel Stezel, and the new arrangement is heard over the radio with increasing frequency....The song... has already sold over 500,000 records with Mr. Dorsey's original arrangements and words" (Ya-zoo, 1041, 4).

A Wizard on the Guitar. Tampa Red's hometown was Tampa, Florida. He was born Hudson Woodbridge in Smithville, Georgia on Janu-ary 8, 1904, although he gives his birth date as December 25, 1908 (Humphrey 1994, 5). He was known throughout his childhood as Hudson Whitaker, taking the family name Whitaker from his grandmother who raised him.

The moniker "Tampa Red," became coupled with the bright red hair for which he was known during his rearing in the city of Tampa, Florida. He was known during the 1920s and 1930s as "The Guitar Wizard." He was famous for the unique slide-guitar style that he developed, a technique expanded by such guitarists as Robert Nighthawk, Chuck Berry, and Duane Allman.

Mark Humphrey describes his virtuosity on the guitar. He is best known for the "bottleneck blues guitar." The sound produced... is described as fluidly vocal, expressively lonesome, sad, sexy, jubi-lant, or angry. It reflected the motif of life for blacks in the South and the North during the Great Depression. Tampa Red performed in the jazz clubs and night clubs of Chicago's Bronzeville neighborhood. He (and a later generation of soul musicians of the 1960s) sang on the streets of Chicago. (Humphrey, "Tampa Red the Guitar Wizard—CD Columbia 1994, 5.)

Tampa Red and Georgia Tom's Partnership. Tampa Red and Georgia Tom continued their partnership into the 1930s, practicing new material for a week before taking it into the studio for recording. Yet Dorsey, while performing with Tampa Red, carried a briefcase filled with his sacred songs, which he would share with churches when they traveled. Dorsey recorded about 40 records as a featured vocalist, and he normally used a pseudonym for these recordings. In his words, he was too lazy to do the vocals, so he gave this task to Tampa Red. He admired Tampa Red most for his beat. Dorsey would later bring that rhythm to gospel music (Yazoo, 1041, 5).

Tampa Red continued to perform as a blues guitarist for the next twenty years, while Dorsey gradually made sacred music his only musical composition. Tampa Red never again enjoyed the popularity he had with Dorsey. In his later years, he helped arriving southern migrants secure food, shelter, and find musical employment. His style was imitated by younger musicians who were successful. Many believed that he lost his motivation (like Dorsey had with the death of his wife Nettie) after his wife Frances died in 1954. His recordings were never of the same quality after her death.

An attempt to rediscover Tampa Red failed in 1961, and he spent many of his last years in obscurity in a nursing home. He died in Chicago on March 19, 1981. Sadly, he was neither mourned nor celebrated for his contributions to blues and his guitar wizardry. He was remembered by pianist Blind Boy Davis "as one of the kingpins of pre-war Chicago blues" (Humphrey, 7).

Secular Success Exacts a Price

Secular success had exacted its price on Thomas Dorsey during this decade, while the sacred flame burned dimly in the recesses of his mind. Did he recall his mother's past prayers and urging to use his talent for God's work? In the author's estimation, the underlying root of Dorsey's first "nervous breakdown," was a conflict between his involvement in both the sacred and secular music dimensions.

His niece, Lena McLin, relates his frustration after his intense religious experience in 1921 at the National Baptist Convention. Dorsey continued to write gospel songs for seven years after his second conversion, which he sent to churches without success. McLin said in the PBS Documentary, "We've Come This Far by Faith," that he mailed the gospel songs he wrote to all the churches he could remember, including stamps for return mail. He received one answer, and then nothing during the next three years (PBS Documentary, "We've Come This Far by Faith," 8).

Dorsey's blues compositions were well-known, but he still preferred the dance halls to the church pews. Nettie had tried unsuccessfully to persuade her husband to use his talents and gifts in service to the Lord. She had to work during the years 1926 to 1928 after Dorsey became unable to create music because of his debilitating illness. Their savings depleted, she worked until his strength returned. The sudden death of a neighbor did nothing to help Dorsey's frame of mind during this period. The man, a young taxi cab driver, became seriously ill, and Dorsey sat with him one night and offered words of comfort. The young man was dead the next morning.

A Crisis of Faith

The death of this young man troubled Dorsey, who couldn't understand how a person could die so quickly when he hadn't been ill for any length of time. The experience inspired him to write the gospel song "If You See My Savior" (Turner, 59). The significance of this song is that Dorsey returned to writing gospel music during a crisis in faith in his life. Composing a gospel song during a crisis in faith would be a motif that he would repeat in 1932.

Dorsey's wife Nettie and her sister had encouraged him to return to God during his two-year illness. He agreed to visit a local minister, Bishop Haley, who was known as a healer. Haley restored his health and faith in God. The minister spoke to him, and allegedly pulled a serpent from his mouth. Dorsey claimed that he felt healed from the encounter, yet doctors had not been able to determine the cause of his illness and weight loss during this time of illness (PBS Documentary, "We've Come This Far by Faith," 7).

Haley spoke prophetically to Dorsey, telling him that God had an assignment on his life. Additionally, he assured Dorsey that the root of the sickness was spiritual and not natural. He was "not as sick in the body as in mind, and if he would use his music for God he would be healed (Boyer, 59)." Dorsey, until that time, hadn't written a gospel song in two years. His last gospel success was the song "If I Don't Get There," Number 117, included in the second revision of Lucie Campbell's edition of the *Gospel Pearls* in 1921 (Boyer, 59). Disappointed that the song didn't become popular and that he didn't gain recognition as a gospel songwriter, Dorsey soon returned to secular music shortly after its composition. He returned to secular music, to the world that had brought him fame and success.

From the Secular to the Sacred

It is apparent that the prophecy of Bishop Haley began to resonate in Dorsey's heart. He began to distance himself from secular music, though he continued to play both jazz and blues throughout the 1930s. Now, the focus shifted to involvement in sacred activities. The 1930s would bring acceptance for his "gospel songs." Church life for Black America would become revolutionized in the way the European Church had been revolutionized by Luther, Calvin, the Anglican Church, and hymnody.

The 1930s was a pivotal decade for Dorsey. God spoke to him clearly in 1932 after the death of his wife Nettie and newborn son. He had elected to travel to St. Louis for a revival. His wife was expecting their first child any day. He got into the car and, realizing that he had forgotten his briefcase, had the opportunity to return and stay home. One of the people who intended to go with him decided instead to remain in Chicago.

He later received a telegram during the service stating that he must hurry home. His wife had just died. Dorsey found her dead when he returned home. He was able to hold his infant son in his arms; however, the baby boy died the next day. Dorsey was inconsolable. He blamed himself for going to the revival and leaving his wife alone. He blamed God for letting his wife and son die. He didn't want to serve God at all. He only wanted to return to secular music.

God intervened by speaking directly to Dorsey. He reminded Dorsey that he had chosen to go to St. Louis when God had given him the chance to return home. Dorsey repented with the words: "Thank you Lord, I understand. I'll never make that same mistake again" (Dorsey, 4). The following Saturday at Madame Malone's Poro College, he was able to compose his most famous song:

> There in my solitude, I began to browse over the keys
> like a gentle herd pasturing on tender turf. Something
> happened to me there. I had a strange feeling inside.
> A sudden calm—a quiet stillness as my fingers began
> to manipulate over keys, words began to fall in place
> on the melody like drops of water falling from the
> crevice of a rock" (Dorsey, 4-5).

This crisis changed the trajectory of Dorsey's life. He now began to live the destiny that God had pre-ordained for His glory. For it is impossible for a true "child of God" to continue to live outside of God's will indefinitely. God's anointing power however, cannot be manifested without a willing and humble spirit, reconciliation, and forgiveness. Indeed, Thomas Dorsey, through his pioneering of the gospel song, fulfilled the purpose for which God gifted him, living out the message of Isaiah 55: 8-11:

> *For my thoughts are not your thoughts, neither are your ways my ways, saith the Lord. For as the heavens are higher than the earth, so are my ways higher than your ways, and my thoughts than your thoughts... So shall my word be that goeth forth out of my mouth: it shall not return unto me void, but it shall accomplish that which I please, and it shall prosper in the thing whereto I sent it (KJV).*

Chapter Two:

Thomas Dorsey's Pre-Gospel Heritage

The "gospel song," the term coined by Thomas A. Dorsey to distinguish his gospel music, has a rich heritage in the body of African American sacred music. This heritage is the direct result of the legacy that enslaved blacks brought with them from West Africa. This oral tradition was embedded in the culture and psyche of the enslaved African people and transmitted to their children and their children's children through song.

Early southern African-American sacred music reflected the outpouring of the sufferings and anguish of the slaves. It included prayer, praise, and preaching. Enslaved Africans became exposed to the songs and preaching of evangelists, including Moody and Sankey, at camp-town revivals. God was revealed there, through those teachings, as a different God from the God presented through the religion taught by the slave owners. Fashioning a theology of liberation and deliverance taken directly from the book of Exodus and the teachings of Jesus Christ, hymns were now composed by the Negro people that identified their personal "God-talk," or theology. Walker (1987) examined twenty-four prayer and praise hymns. These hymns were developed during the period from 1885 to 1925, following Reconstruction, but before the advent of gospel music (Wise, 2002). They belong to the period defined as Euro hymns with black rhythm and were known as "hymns of improvisation." Appendix IV lists the periods of black sacred music development (Walker 1979). Walker makes this conclusion about the relevance of this body of religious music [prayer and praise hymns] in Volume I of his work *Spirits That Dwell in Deep Woods* (1987):

> They belong in the genre of black religious folk music. These songs are still sung in the South. [Their] origin stems from the prayer meetings and pre-service devotionals of Black religious life (Walker, 1979).

Early Hymns of Prayer and Praise

The twenty-four hymns are analyzed individually from four different perspectives: their biblical basis, their theological mooring, their lyric form; and their contemporary significance (Walker, 1979). Some of the prayer and praise hymns made their way into the devotional services and revival meetings of Pentecostal and Baptist churches in the North. The hymns, like all black sacred music, were adapted and changed by those who sang them. For example, "Another Day's Journey and I'm So Glad" became "It's Another Day's Journey and I'm Glad." On the other hand, hymns such as "Glory, Glory, Hallelujah," "I Want to Be Ready," "Jesus Is a Rock in a Weary Land" and "Jesus Is on the Main Line" remained virtually unchanged. Most of those hymns, however, are now lost or known only to the rural southern elders who heard them sung by their ancestors. Twenty-first century musicians are virtually unaware of this genre of black sacred music and of their own Levitical heritage.

Thomas Dorsey lived at a time and place when this music was sung in family gatherings, prayer meetings, and at church devotions. The oral tradition, preserved from Africa, was sustained through the moans, chants, and rhythms that enslaved Africans brought from their homeland to America, and it is largely for that reason that a body of black sacred music existed in the Negro community after Reconstruction. The invisible church of the slaves became visible after the Civil War, and it grew during Reconstruction, marrying the European hymns of Isaac Watts and Charles Wesley to its own improvisations. Dorsey drew upon this rich heritage as a gospel composer. He shares his memories of this part of his pre-gospel heritage:

> I went to school in a one-room building. They taught three grades in that room. We used to sing all the songs there. That's going back to 1905. I used to like the Watts hymns. He was a good hymn-writer. I loved the meaning and the feeling of hymns like "Must Jesus Bear the Cross Alone"? (Turner, 63).

Later, the lessons, stories, and songs Dorsey learned in the rural church, school, and on the family front porch in Villa Rica would contrast sharply with the urban lessons of Atlanta, Philadelphia, Gary, and Chicago. Nevertheless, he would eventually return to his roots. He explained in an interview:

> I always had rhythm in my bones. I like the solid beat. I like the long moaning, groaning tone. I like the rock. You know how they rock and shout in the church? It's a thing people look for now (Broughton, 29).

Dorsey's Developmental Influences

Two gospel composers most identified with Dorsey's development as composers were Charles Albert Tindley (1851-1933) and Lucie E. Campbell Williams (1885-1963). Tindley, the self-taught son of slaves, was born in Berlin, Maryland, where he established his first congregation. He moved to Philadelphia in 1875 and was employed as "a hod carrier and a sexton" at the John Wesley Methodist Episcopal Church (the Methodist Episcopal Church) [which] would become the United Methodist Church in 1970 (Boyer, 27).

Tindley, who later became a United Methodist bishop, was deeply influenced by the worship of the Sanctified Church. His musical compositions borrowed heavily from their rhythms. Tindley was one of the most influential composers and pastors of his time. His church, the Bainbridge Street Methodist Episcopal Church, became one of the largest churches in Philadelphia, and his musical compositions were performed there. Acknowledged as "The Father of the Gospel Hymn," Tindley's songs were first published in 1901.

In 1922, he established the group The Tindley Gospel Singers, accompanied by a piano (Turner, 117). The Civil Rights Movement adapted one of his hymns, "I'll Overcome Someday" (Kemp, 2011, 22). The song, renamed "We Shall Overcome Someday," became the Movement's rallying song. Other compositions, "Leave It There" and "Stand by Me," remain standards in sacred black music compositions. Tindley also encouraged other musicians to adapt and use his compositions.

Lucie E. Campbell. Lucie Eddie Campbell was the female composer who helped increase the circulation of Dorsey's music in church worship services. Born in Duck Hill, Mississippi, she was the youngest of eleven children born to former slaves Burrell and Isabella Wilkerson Campbell. Her father was killed by a train shortly after her birth, and her mother, in search of better job opportunities, moved her children to Memphis, Tennessee. Campbell attended elementary and high school there, graduating as valedictorian of her high school class in 1899. Her record was so impressive that she was immediately hired as a teacher. She served as Music Director of the Sunday School and

Baptist Training Union for the National Baptist Convention. Each year, she wrote a new song for the youth choir she directed. (Reagon, 118). More than fifty of her songs have become gospel standards. Among them are the beloved "He Understands, He'll Say Well Done," and her shout song, "Jesus Gave Me Water" (Boyer 139,140). Campbell also was an influential member of The National Sunday School Board of the National Baptist Convention's music committee. *The Gospel Pearls* hymnbook, launched at the convention in 1921, was Dorsey's first national exposure.

Dorsey and Campbell met in 1930 at the National Baptist Convention. Campbell's songs gradually incorporated some of the Chicago sound of gospel characterized by Dorsey, Kenneth Morris, Roberta Martin, Sallie Martin, and Mahalia Jackson. Her songs were a bridge between the hymnody of the 1900s and the new gospel song popularized by Dorsey. She remains a major songwriter within the gospel tradition.

The "Father of Gospel Music"

Thomas Dorsey was well aware of compositions by other black composers in the gospel tradition, even as he invented his own version of the gospel hymn. In addressing the question of whether Tindley or Dorsey rightfully deserves the title "The Father of Gospel Music," Dr. Clayton Hannah, who worked closely with Dorsey during the 1980s, makes this distinction between the two composers: Charles Tindley is "The Father of Black Hymnody," and Thomas Dorsey is "The Father of Gospel Music." As his rationale, Hannah refers to the international appeal of Dorsey's work, as well as the fact that ministers commonly wrote pieces for their congregations. Tindley, as pastor, spent the majority of his time as shepherd to his flock. It was common for pastors to write music for their personal congregations and to teach them the music. This was seen more often, however, in Pentecostal worship practices, where the music was rarely written down or copyrighted. The influence of Dorsey's music spread much farther than that of Tindley's during his lifetime. "Dorsey," Hannah stated emphatically, "wrote for the world" (*Gospelrama* News Vol.3, No. 9, September 1982, Washington, DC).

Arguing that gospel music existed prior to Dorsey's coining the term "gospel song," some critics claim that the term "gospel song" originated with British composers of the nineteenth century:

> … the songwriter Phillip Bliss, who, in 1874, put together a printed collection titled Gospel Songs to distinguish them from either Psalms or hymns. Ira. D. Sankey, Dwight L. Moody's music director, had heard the phrase "to sing the gospel" during an evangelistic tour of Britain (Turner, 53).

Dorsey rebuts this claim in an interview in which he gives his analysis of the difference between his gospel songs and other hymns. "I created the style," he says (Turner, 64). He elaborates further on the point:

> …In the first place, they [my songs] had a beat. Some of them had a tempo. Some had simple good news. They weren't written in flowery English that was so high that the ignorant people couldn't understand. It was just time for change (Turner, 64).

Dorsey makes a further clarification about the difference of his music and other "gospel" music in an interview from TADS 27 January 18, 1977:

> Now I didn't originate the word "gospel." I want you to
> know. Didn't originate that word. Gospel, the word
> "gospel" has been used down through the ages. But I
> took the word, took a group of singers, or one singer,
> as far as that's concerned, and I embellished [gospel],
> made it beautiful, more noticeable, and more suscep-
> tible with runs and trills and moans in it. That's really
> one of the reasons my folk call it "gospel music" (Har-
> ris, 1992, 151).

Dorsey understood that only God's will could govern gospel music: its creation and acceptance. He stated: "Nothing will take the place of gospel music...somebody might do it differently or add something to it, but any power in the music comes from God...and it's all about what God wants" (*The Voice*, 1982, 94). Turner, however, ascribes commercial gain as the prime motivation for Dorsey's music:

> Even if Dorsey didn't coin the term [gospel music],
> he was the person who saw the commercial potential
> of a form of music that was contemporary in sound
> and sense, orthodox in theology, and capable of be-
> ing sung in performance rather than only as an act of
> worship (54).

Dorsey's Gospel Song: "The Christian Fruit of an African Root"

In Walker's words, [gospel music] is "the Christian fruit of an African root." It was the sum total of knowledge gained from existing in two worlds—one black and one white. Thomas Dorsey brought his total experience of this duality into the genre which became known as gospel music. His unique contribution sparked a grassroots movement that grew outside of the established black church experience. It conferred legitimacy on the black sacred musical eras known as "historic gospel" and "early gospel." Dorsey described his creation in these words:

> This rhythm that I had, I brought with me to gospel songs. I was a blues singer, and I carried that with me into the gospel songs. These songs were not just written. Something had to happen, something had to be done; there had to be a feeling. They just weren't printed and distributed. Somebody had to feel something, somebody had to hand down light for mankind's pathway, smooth the road and the rugged way, give him courage, bring the black man peace, joy, and happiness. Gospel songs come from prayer, meditation, hard times, and pain. But they are written out of divine memories, out of the feelings in your soul (Broughton, 43).

Thomas Dorsey benefitted from the work of those who preceded him. He, in turn, developed a genre and students who demonstrated and shared his compositions. Those disciples reflected and broadened the musical style he brought into the church from his own early musical training and, later, his blues and jazz repertoires. Those innovations made possible the advances in the gospel music of the twentieth and twenty-first centuries.

Chapter Three:

Thomas Dorsey as a Modern-Day Levite

T he first unofficial biographer of Thomas A. Dorsey, Ruth Smith, lauded him as a poet and as a shepherd, drawing parallels between his music and ministry and that of King David in the Hebrew Bible, whose musical prowess was used many times to counteract the "evil spirits" that God inflicted on King Saul. He was called a "man after God's own heart" (1 Samuel 13:14; Acts 13:22, [KJV]). God chose him as his servant. David pleased God, even though he had to be disciplined for his unrighteousness.

David supplied the design and acquired the materials Solomon used to build the temple for God in Jerusalem. He began the Levitical order of worship later instituted by Solomon in Second Chronicles and re-instituted in Nehemiah. He was renowned as a poet and composer. He was a mighty warrior who led his people to countless victories over their enemies. Psalm 78:72 reads: "He fed them according to the integrity of his heart; and guided them by the skillfulness of his hands" (KJV).

Thomas Dorsey's legacy as a shepherd shares similarities with the priestly (Old Testament Levitical) legacy when viewed through the lens of the musical organization he co-founded in 1933: The National Convention of Gospel Choirs and Choruses (NCGCC). It is the oldest black music convention in America and is dedicated to preserving Dorsey's music and heritage and to training youth for service in church ministry. Broughton writes of the prophetic nature of Thomas

33

Dorsey's gospel song and emphasizes his prophetic influence on gospel music:

> Thomas A. Dorsey is the grand old man of gospel music. No one has had a greater influence on gospel singing; no one has been quite as prophetic; no one spans the entire history of gospel music quite like Dorsey. More than any other individual, Thomas A. Dorsey is gospel, and his story is the story of gospel (29).

Dorsey and Divine Inspiration

A prophet, biblically, is the spokesperson of God. A prophet is God's servant. Prophets are visionary. They speak by divine inspiration, exhorting the people. The Old Testament gives many examples of the prophetic gift. Thomas Dorsey spoke of his practice of meditating to receive divine inspiration. He said that his gospel music was "written out of divine memories, out of the feelings in your soul" (Broughton, 43).

The Bible records messages delivered through God's prophets and prophetesses to his chosen people. Prophets also used music for divine inspiration. Samuel had several schools of prophecy, where music was the instrument that allowed prophets to meditate with God. The purpose of the music was to transport the prophets into a "state of ecstasy" (1 Samuel 10: 1-8 [KJV]). Music is a universal language, a gift that God has given to His people from creation. Dorsey uses these words to describe its power:

> Music has something that will draw; it has something that will soothe; it has something that will attract; it has something that will get inside a person quicker than anything else. It can do you more good than a pint of medicine (Turner, 64).

Smith identifies the music of Thomas Dorsey as prophetic from Pauline epistles. The New Testament definition of a prophet is one who proclaims the Word of God. Paul writes in Ephesians 3:5 that the "mystery of Christ is now revealed by the Spirit." Paul states further in 1 Corinthians 14:3 that the purpose of prophecy is to "edify, encourage, and comfort" the people. That is a function of the preached gospel. It is also experienced in the lyrics of the sung gospel penned by Thomas A. Dorsey. He is credited with writing more than 400 sacred compositions in his lifetime. Dorsey believes he has the good news: gospel. In his words:

> I'm real gospel. If you're gonna define gospel, take
> the King James Version of the Bible, and it'll tell you
> that gospel is good news. That's all it is. It's good
> news coming to you that makes you happy, helps you
> to be saved and helps you surmount all of life's prob-
> lems. About all we need is good news. All we get in
> the newspapers and on the radio and television is bad
> news (Turner, 64).

Composers use the prophetic gift in songwriting; some use biblical texts exclusively. While Dorsey's music didn't explicitly quote biblical texts, it spoke of the presence of the divine in times of personal pain. Prophecy is addressed through Dorsey's lyrical compositions, which address one's personal relationship to God and the righteousness necessary to inherit the Kingdom of Heaven.

Dorsey as Prophet

Dorsey wrote from a personal theology of faith, hope, and God's presence in times of depression, oppression, sadness, and pain. He spoke of a better future life—far removed from the troubles of the

35

present. He wrote of a Jesus who was there, of a Lord who was present in the storm. He spoke of a God who cared about one's struggles, calling his music "songs with a message." He usually gave credit in the written sheet music to the singer or singers and often appended a personal message about the song's meaning. Those prophetic lessons are shared through his songs, poems, and teaching.

Dorsey was convicted to write gospel music because he felt it was the Lord's will for his life, even when his music was rejected by churches. He felt God's hand upon him. He relied on God's strength and was empowered by this belief. At age 70, he shared this observation in this quotation:

> I kept pushing gospel because, somehow, I knew I was right. I knew I was the one the Master wanted to do it, and I did it. I was richly rewarded for my persistence. I've traveled and performed all over the world, and I've heard my songs sung in lots of different languages. I've gotten a lot of satisfaction in my long life. (Muwakkil, "The Father of Gospel Music" *The Reader*, 30).

Dorsey as Shepherd

There are many attributes used to describe a shepherd in the Bible. The International Standard Bible Encyclopedia, 2006, defines a shepherd in this manner: "(shep'-erd) (ro±eh, ro±l; poimen, "one who tends flocks." The Twenty-Third Psalm is a beautiful illustration of God as our shepherd. Easton's Bible Dictionary, enlarges that definition to include the function of a pastor as seen in Jeremiah 3:15: "And I will give you pastors according to mine heart, which shall feed you with knowledge and understanding" (KJV).

The Bible portrays God as the Shepherd Leader of Israel. The New Testament depicts Jesus as the "Good Shepherd," John 10:14: "I am the good shepherd, and know my sheep, and am known of mine" (KJV). Jesus the Christ is ultimately portrayed as the Chief Shepherd we meet in the next life (1 Peter 5:4). "And when the chief Shepherd shall appear, ye shall receive a crown of glory that fadeth not away" (KJV). Jesus is also called the great shepherd that God raised from the dead. Hebrews 13:20 states: "Now the God of peace that brought again from the dead our Lord Jesus, that great shepherd of the sheep, through the blood of the everlasting covenant (KJV)."

How then does Dorsey's biographer Ruth Smith compare Dorsey, the man, to the good shepherd, the shepherd king, the chief shepherd, or the shepherd leader in her biography? She offers the following analysis of his calling to write gospel music: He is "the twentieth-century David, who was chosen like Moses, Joshua, or David to be instrumental in leading them out ..." (Smith, 1935, 47).

This reference is to the attitude of the African American community in the 1930s, and Smith's inference that blacks had forgotten God after World War I and abandoned their spiritual roots. During that period, they had lost the deep faith of their ancestors. Church for them was a show and a sham from the pulpit, to the choir, to the worshipper. It was then that God decided to call Dorsey "from his waywardness and put him in readiness for the role he must play," she says (Smith, 47).

Smith characterizes Dorsey as taking care of his heavenly father's sheep by "leading his flock of singers with songs into green pasture... messages that calm and encourage...[that] keep them from stampeding" (Smith, 47). In continuing the analogy, Dorsey is David, singing and playing before ministers and congregations to relieve them of the evil God allowed because of their waywardness, as David played before Saul.

Dorsey as a Spiritual Warrior

Dorsey is the giant slayer fighting the forces within the church. He resists the spiritual strongholds of the fruits of pride and heaviness that sap the life energy of the people. Smith places him in the solitude needed to pray and compose when he is pursued by his own private demons. While he is there, God supplies him with the peace and strength that enables him to stand against the preachers who refuse to allow his music in their churches (Smith, 52). These largely were mainline "silk stocking" African American churches in the 1920s that had no tolerance for the music of Thomas Dorsey and that were content to sing arranged spirituals, jubilee songs, anthems, and hymns. During this period however, there also existed singing evangelists, usually accompanied by guitar with blues rhythms and preachers who had established followings through the "race records" marketed by record companies.

The songs that Dorsey wrote during these periods of solitude include "Hide Me in Thy Bosom, Jesus" and "He Brought Me All the Way." Smith describes him as a spiritual warrior fighting for the maintenance of a spiritual kingdom. David was a natural warrior fighting for the cause of a natural kingdom (Smith, 52).

Music scholar Tony Heilbut refers to gospel music as "good news and bad times" (Walker, 1979, 127). Dorsey has always referred to the "gospel song" as the "Good News of the New Testament" (Turner, 63). Noted musicologist Boyer asserts, "There has been no more imposing figure in gospel than Thomas Andrew Dorsey, and for his contributions to the music, he was named early on 'Father of African-American Gospel Music' (Boyer, 61)."

Dorsey and the Black Church

Educated blacks of the twentieth century had begun to use hymn-books for religious services. The Methodist and Baptist denominations had invested money in these books. Choirs had been formed to sing and lead the congregants, who were not as literate as others in the proper rendition of the hymns, as pastors sought to move away from the emotionalism and exuberance of black southern worship traditions. Restraint was encouraged in worship. Boyer discusses this phenomenon in the PBS Documentary, "We've Come This Far by Faith—Part 3":

> There was the feeling that the more white you acted, the more you would be accepted by white people. There was not that kind of pride about having lived through slavery, up in the early part of the century. So that the whole emphasis was ridding every Negro of everything that was Negroid, including the food, including the clothing, and here, including the church service ritual. So all of a sudden, now, we get Brahms and we get Handel. And everybody loves Brahms and Handel, particularly those who created Brahms and Handel. And here we begin to get a whole conflict between the way people are going to worship. And many preachers said, don't sing those slave songs altogether. (Boyer, 5).

The Methodist AME churches had used hymnbooks since the beginning of the twentieth century. The Baptists followed suit and began to publish their own hymnbooks such as *The Gospel Pearls*, published in 1921. In 1928, the National Baptist Convention published the book of spirituals *Spirituals Triumphant*. Departing from this practice, however, most of the African American Pentecostal religions didn't use hymnbooks for their service, relying more heavily on "singing in the spirit." The Church of God in Christ, however, during this period, developed a hymnbook for worship services.

These changes [gospel songs] in liturgical practices and church worship disturbed and displaced many elders in the Baptist church, who felt that they and their religious heritage were being devalued in northern cities. In light of this, Thomas Dorsey arguably appeared on the scene as a modern-day David slaying Goliath when he took a stand against the status quo of the Black Church.

Those battles with churches that refused to accept his music forced Dorsey to work outside the established church. This led to the later grassroots work of Sallie Martin and others within his circle that spread the good news of the gospel through his songs. It was from these humble beginnings that a national organization arose. Two large mainline black Baptist churches in Chicago, however, did accept his music in the early 1930s. They were Ebenezer Missionary Baptist Church and Pilgrim Baptist Church.

Ebenezer and Pilgrim Baptist Churches

Ebenezer Missionary Baptist Church was the first church in Chicago to organize a gospel choir, and it was established in 1931 under the directorship of Professor Theodore Frye and pianist, Professor Thomas Dorsey. Rev. Junius Austin, Sr., Pastor of Pilgrim Baptist Church, subsequently asked Dorsey to organize a gospel choir at Pilgrim, which was organized in 1932. Thus, the two choirs were both organized within months of each other. Ebenezer member Yvonne Salter characterizes the efforts in these words: "Ebenezer is the birthplace of gospel music. Pilgrim is the home of gospel music" (Salter Interview, 2014).

40

Ebenezer and Pilgrim have similar histories. Both were ornate Jewish synagogues in the 1930s, and both have achieved landmark status. In addition, the two had large populations during the Great Migration and had instituted programs to educate migrants and social programs for neighborhood children. Both also suffered membership attrition during the latter decades of the twentieth century. "The church has endured so much and struggles to bring the community back to church. The task in the twenty-first century is bringing in the young to carry on. Now with landmark status, the church must go on," says Salter (Salter Interview).

On January 6, 2006, Pilgrim Baptist Church was destroyed by a fire that occurred as a result of roofing repairs, and numerous gospel treasures were lost. The church continues to worship in a building they own across the street from the original structure. Arnold Sevier remembers those losses to history: "We were still across the street then. They had music from 1915. I can't describe the feeling I had when I found out there was a fire... There were the old vintage pianos...all that music... (Personal Interview)."

Despite the acceptance of Dorsey's music at Ebenezer and Pilgrim Baptist Churches, there were those at both churches who were not in favor of the new music. Professor Edward Boatner, the director of the Senior Choir at Pilgrim, was a classically trained composer and singer. He was highly regarded as an arranger of spirituals. He served in an official capacity with The National Baptist Convention. Boatner later left Pilgrim and moved to New York. He had great animosity toward Thomas Dorsey and his musical program. Boatner had been hired by the new pastor, Junius Austin, Sr., in 1925 to provide worship services with more restraint and less emotion. Consequently, he was unhappy with the change made by that same pastor in 1932.

Austin, Pilgrim's pastor, however, was concerned about his flock, and he saw, firsthand, the burdens his people were facing with the Great Depression. He wanted music to lift them up and encourage them, and he had heard Dorsey's music at an anniversary program when Ebenezer's choir visited Pilgrim. Dorsey had originally joined Pilgrim in 1919 under the leadership of the former pastor, Dr. S.E. J. Watson. Smith now wanted Dorsey back home. Upon Dorsey's return, he formed Pilgrim's first gospel chorus. It was an immediate success. People enthusiastically joined the choir, and also joined the church, boosting its membership. Pilgrim's services were spirit-filled once again. Church attendance continued to increase steadily after the Depression, and services were eventually broadcast by speaker throughout the neighborhood.

"Historic Gospel"

Walker (1979) connected gospel's widespread appeal with the tough economic conditions:

> Gospel music, at bottom, is religious folk music that is clearly identifiable with the social circumstance of the black community in America. The authenticity of folkways and folk expressions (including music) can be gauged by how closely they mirror the experience of the group. Gospel music does precisely that, in very much the same manner as does its early predecessor, the spiritual. Gospel music, then, is an individual expression of a collective experience, in a religious context (Walker, 1991, 138).

Dorsey's music, in other words, spoke to the people's hearts, made them feel better in a worship service with songs sung with a

42

beat. Walker refers to this time period as "Historic Gospel." It is the poetic music of the Depression that clearly echoes the sentiments in people's hearts. Dorsey also reminded those who bought his music that the words revealed the difference between sacred and secular lyrics. Smith characterizes the sacred meaning of his gospel songs that carry a message:

> They are the fruits of a divinely inspired mind...they carry a message, and the message is made the more appealing because of the music that accompanies it. His songs have messages of persuasion; expressions of conversion, perseverance through adversity by prayer; joys of being a Christian; songs looking forward to our heavenly reward (Smith, 55).

Dorsey's Music Is Finally Accepted

Thanks to a powerful woman of God, Mother Willie Mae Ford Smith, from St. Louis, Missouri, the rejection of Dorsey's gospel songs came to an end in the 1930s. Dorsey attended the Jubilee Session of the National Baptist Convention held in Chicago to sell the music to "If You See My Savior." He also sold the song published in the *Gospel Pearls* in 1921, "Someday, Somewhere." To his surprise and elation, he heard "If You See My Savior" booming from the Coliseum's speakers. People were lying in the aisles, overcome by the Holy Spirit. Dorsey convinced the convention managers to let him to set up a booth to sell his music to all who were interested.

Eventually, Dorsey's crusade for acceptance of his music would culminate in a national organization that would one day simply be known as "The Dorsey Convention," founded by Dorsey, Sallie Martin, Magnolia Butts, and Theodore Frye in 1933. It germinated from an initial meeting at Metropolitan Community Church, where Magnolia Butts was the choir's directress. Dorsey called Frye and Butts together to organize a choral union that would bring gospel choirs together. The first meeting resulted in the formation of a city-wide gospel chorus. It was named the National Convention of Gospel Choirs, Choruses and Smaller Musical Groups, Inc. The national organization (NCGCC) followed within a year.

Dorsey's compositions gained popularity through modeled demonstrations of the way the songs should be delivered. He trained soloists, trios, and quartets to sing in his style and established a national "gospel music circuit." He maintained strict control of his music. Record companies were barred from recording or copyrighting his compositions, and buyers of his music could not sing it for commercial profit. Such restrictions were motivated by well-earned lessons from his days in the secular arena, where he witnessed the unscrupulous business practices imposed on musicians by the record companies.

Dorsey's entrepreneurial roots, as a boy, were planted in Atlanta's urban environment. This knowledge developed into the creation of a full-time music copywriting and publishing enterprise, the first black-owned music publishing company established in Chicago during the 1930s. He wrote books on poetry and choir decorum, published his own gospel songs, and helped to launch many careers for blacks in the music industry.

Dorsey's "Disciples"

The three singers most closely identified with Dorsey's gospel style are Sallie Martin, Roberta Martin (no relation to Sallie), and Mahalia Jackson. Evangelist Willie Mae Ford Smith became indispensable in promoting the legacy of the National Convention of Gospel Choirs and Choruses, and she is best known for her work with the creation and training of soloists for music ministry within the Dorsey organization.

Sallie Martin. Sallie Martin (1896-1988) was born in Pittsfield, Georgia. She arrived in Chicago in 1927 with her husband and small son. On weekdays, she worked as a domestic, but on Sundays she was a church singer. After settling in Chicago, she chose the Sanctified Church and left her former membership with the Baptist Church. Sallie Martin didn't read music, but she improvised the songs through the power of the Holy Spirit.

Martin, upon her exposure to Thomas Dorsey's music, wanted to work with him. She devised a plan to meet him by arranging to appear on programs and to sing solos at local churches where he also was scheduled for an appearance. When her opportunity to sing came, she would sing the audience into frenzy. Finally, in 1929, she was introduced to Dorsey by Millie Dennis. She auditioned for him three times before he accepted her. The rejections were a result of her inability to read music and the lack of polish in her voice. Nonetheless, Theodore Frye encouraged Dorsey to take her on.

Thus, Martin became Dorsey's first "disciple," and he trained her in his style. She became a part of the Thomas A. Dorsey Gospel Singers Trio, formed in 1932 to demonstrate his songs. Later, in 1934, she joined his quartet that also featured Bertha Armstrong, Dettie Gay, and Mattie Wilson (Boyer, 58). Martin wasn't assigned a solo until the next year (Boyer, 63), and the rest is history, as she toured religious circuits singing, promoting, and selling Dorsey's music.

Martin also organized Dorsey's publishing business, The Dorsey House of Music, which began in 1932 (Walker, 149). Her beginning weekly salary for the responsibility was $4.00. She challenged Dorsey to raise it to $5.00 if she showed a profit, a testament to her business acumen. Salaries had dropped in all occupations after the Depression. Sallie

Martin trusted God in her decision to quit her job, which included room and board to work with Dorsey.

> She knew how to market sheet music, save on print-
> ing, charge for voice lessons, and save money.
> Dorsey [began] delegating such responsibilities to
> Martin once their partnership was solidified. She
> organized his music store, hired assistants to work at
> the counter, and kept records of the inventory. After
> a few short months she was able to show a profit for
> his business (Boyer, 63).

Martin's Business Acumen. Up to that time, Dorsey had never been able to make his business profitable, and the two clashed over policy. Martin knew that profits would only be increased with increased sales. She remarked on this fact in the 1983 documentary "Say Amen Somebody," where she revealed that Dorsey's business success was mainly due to her administrative skills. Although Martin was extremely instrumental in Dorsey's music publishing business, he kept the enterprise under his own control. Astutely, Dorsey linked his organization, The National Convention of Gospel Choirs and Choruses, to his publishing house. The music was sold not only on the streets, at engagements, conventions, and at his church visits, but also at the annual gospel music conventions.

Martin also brought her administrative skills to the convention, becoming the NCGCC's first secretary. In addition to convention duties, she toured the country singing Dorsey's music, selling sheet music, and organizing unions and choruses. Martin, as first national organizer for the convention, was charged with organizing choruses, choirs, glee clubs, quartets, sextets, octets, and unions, in whatever church community in the United States and elsewhere. She also had to report on all the work she had accomplished at each year's convention.

Sallie Martin also was a songwriter and gospel promoter who wrote the gospel hit "How About You?" She became a gospel concert artist, with Ruth Jones as her pianist. Jones later became known as the secular artist Dinah Washington. In 1940 Sallie Martin and Kenneth Morris, opened Martin and Morris Music, Inc., with the backing of Rev. Clarence Cobb, pastor of First Church of Deliverance in Chicago. It was there at First Church of Deliverance that Morris, the organist, introduced the Hammond B3 organ to churches and musicians.

The Sallie Martin Singers. That same year, Martin and Morris decided to organize a singing group, similar to those of Thomas Dorsey and Roberta Martin, to advertise their inventory. The group was known as The Sallie Martin Singers, whose early members were Dorothy Simmons, Sarah Daniels, Julia Mae Smith, and Melva Williams, accompanied on piano by Ruth Jones. Martin adopted Cora Brewer, who joined the group in 1942. Martin toured with them throughout the United States and Europe until 1975. Martin, during the year 1960, was estimated to be wealthier than Mahalia Jackson or Roberta Martin, who were also Dorsey disciples (Boyer, 63).

The group's signature sound was the "unrefined, uneven, and yet warm tone of Sallie and the brilliant alto of Cora" (Boyer, 92). The group gained notoriety in 1944 under the name of "The Sallie Martin Colored Ladies Quartet," and Martin was known to "rock the house" (Boyer, 93). The group headlined a performance at a crusade by the then well-known evangelist Aimee Semple McPherson. Differences arose that dissolved the partnership between Sallie Martin and Kenneth Morris.

During the early civil rights movement, Martin actively support-ed the ministry of Dr. Martin Luther King, Jr., representing him at Nige-ria's opening 1960 independence ceremony. She contributed to the Nigerian Health Program, and an office building in Isslu-UKA, Nigeria was named in her honor (Boyer, 64).

Martin remained active in the NCGCC until Dorsey retired from composing in the 1980s, where she served as the organization's chair-man of Trustees and National Organizer. After severing her musical part-nership with Dorsey, she moved her membership and service to the First Church of Deliverance. First Church of Deliverance honored Martin for her half-century of service to that church.

Martin received many accolades in her long life. Among them were a Doctorate in Divinity for the Ministry in Gospel Music, awarded by The Metropolitan Churches of Christ, Inc. She was selected as an hon-oree into the American Music and Entertainment Hall of Fame—Gospel Festival in Chicago, along with Thomas A. Dorsey, Dr. Milton Brunson and the Thompson Community Singers in 1982 (*Chicago Defender*, (August 30, 1982, 16). Her stage credits include an appearance in the Paris, France, production of the Gospel Music Extravaganza "Caravans" in 1979, and an appearance in the film "The Power of the Gospel Song" with Thomas A Dorsey.

Martin also participated in a television special with Dorsey and Dr. Clayton Hannah, Gospel Historian (*Chicago Defender*, 16). The event took place at the Chicago Stadium on August 30, 1982 (Fisk Ar-chive material). She was bestowed the title "Mother of Gospel" by the NCGCC. James Cleveland referred to her as the one who "blazed the trail for gospel music when it wasn't a popular art form" (*Ebony Maga-zine*, March 1986, 78).

Roberta Martin. Roberta Martin (1907-1969) was one of six children born to William and Anna Winston in Helena, Arkansas. The family moved to Cairo, Illinois, before settling in Chicago, where Martin played for Sunday school at the tender age of ten. Martin, inspired by her teacher at Wendell Phillips High School in Chicago, originally had dreamed of being a concert pianist. That aspiration changed, however, after she became a gospel convert, which resulted from her appointment as pianist for Ebenezer's Young People's Choir (Boyer, 66). Martin had been exposed to gospel earlier in her life, before she met her mentor Thomas Dorsey. She relates:

> I had been playing at churches nearly all of my life, ever since I was so high. I started down at Pilgrim, where I was the pianist for the Sunday school. At that time I was just interested in church hymns, anthems, choir music, and secular were not exactly gospel songs. The first time I heard gospel singing as such, was this lady and the men–Bertha Wise and her Singers [from Augusta, Georgia]. Miss Wise played the piano for them. They came to our church, and oh, did we enjoy them. Actually, they were famous—they would go around to the National Baptist Convention and sing. They were not exactly gospel songs, but spirituals like gospel songs, and the one that interested me the most was "I Can Tell the World About This." This was in 1933 [1932] (Boyer, 66).

Martin's experience with Dorsey and Frye propelled her into the gospel ministry of song, and she and Frye organized the Martin-Frye Quartet in 1933. By 1935, the name was changed to The Roberta Martin Singers. The young boys from Pilgrim Baptist and Ebenezer Missionary Baptist churches—Eugene Smith, James Lawrence, Robert Anderson, Willie Webb, and Norsalus McKissick—were the original Roberta Martin Singers.

In the 1940s, Bessie Folk and Delois Barrett Campbell were added to the group. Martin traveled, sang, and accompanied the group on piano until the late 1960s, during which time her energy was focused on writing, arranging, and managing her publishing business. An earlier group formed between Roberta and Sallie Martin—The Martin and Martin Singers—was short-lived, and the two singers continued their musical careers separately.

Martin's style was much more refined than that of Thomas Dorsey. The fire of Pentecostal shouters appealed to her, and her genius lay in her ability to "capture their zest with well-modulated voices" (Boyer, 68). Martin also was known for her musical talent as a pianist, wherein she displayed nuance and refinement. Her chords were well-structured—dif-ferent from the bluesy chords of Dorsey; they reflected her earlier clas-sical intentions, and her borrowing from the European classical style. Boyer says:

> She emphasized the first beat of each musical unit in the middle of the piano and provided her own response by answering this beat with secondary beats at the upper ranges of the keyboard. One of her trademarks was bringing a song to a "ritard" (slowing down) at the end, followed by cascading chords all the way to the upper extremes of the keyboard (Boyer, 68).

Martin was also known for reintroducing the call and response technique—symbolic of the Negro spiritual—into her group's singing style by beginning a tradition where each member was both a lead and a background singer. "This practice," Boyer reflected, "encouraged the audience to pay more attention to the delivery of the text and melody by the lead singer. This technique worked well....Martin returned to the original Pentecostal/Negro spiritual practice of call and response with the background voices spurring the leader on to a vocal frenzy" (Boyer, 68).

Martin, an articulate and influential ambassador for gospel music, was featured in "Spirit of an Era—Museum of Natural History," sponsored by the Smithsonian Performing Arts Program in Black American Culture, February 6-8, 1981. She was honored for her achievements in gospel music by a concert and colloquium in 1983 at the Smithsonian Institute (Boyer, 69). Professor Clayton Hannah shares this assessment of her talent:

> [She is] one who made the greatest contribution to gospel music, whose sound was dominant. She was inspired by Thomas A. Dorsey and Sallie Martin, yet combined several styles of black music: the moan, Dorsey bounce, and sanctified syncopation in what became "classic gospel music (*Gospelrama News*, Vol.3, No. 9, September 1982, 5)."

Nevertheless, Roberta Martin has never received the attention deserved for her impact on gospel music. The group had many best sellers during her career. Tony Cummings, the music editor for *Cross Rhythms*, made this observation concerning her legacy: "It's a shame, therefore, that Malaco Records, the company who bought the rights to the vast Savoy catalogue, has served the memory of The Roberta Martin Singers so badly. While another gospel matriarch featured on those 1998 postage stamps, Mahalia Jackson, currently has 139 albums listed on iTunes, Roberta's sole listing is the 1999 CD compilation, "The Best of the Roberta Martin Singers." (www.CrossRhythms. co.uk) Wednesday 25th December 2013). (Four thirty-two cents stamps issued on July 15, 1998 honored the four queens of gospel music: Mahalia Jackson, Clara Ward, Sister Rosetta Tharpe, and Roberta Martin).

At Martin's death, more than 50,000 people paid tribute to her legacy at Mt. Pisgah Baptist Church in Chicago, where she had served as its musical director from 1950 to 1968 (Broughton, 59).

Mahalia Jackson. Known internationally, Mahalia Jackson (1911-1972) became the "gospel superstar" of the 1950s and claimed the undisputed title as the "Queen of Gospel." She was the only child of Rev. Johnny Jackson, Jr., and Charity Clark. She grew up in the Plymouth Rock Baptist Church in New Orleans, Louisiana, and began singing in church at the age of four, according to biographer Laurraine Goreau (Boyer, 83). By the age of ten, she was invited to sing solos in the Junior Choir of the Mount Moriah Baptist Church. The impact of the singing style she heard from the sanctified church down the street from her home, however, would become her hallmark. Jackson, in her 1966 autobiography, remarked:

> I know now that a great influence in my life was the sanctified or holiness churches we had in the South. I was always a Baptist, but there was a sanctified church right next to our house in New Orleans. Those people had no choir and no organ. They used the drum, the cymbal, the tambourine, and the steel triangle. Everybody in there sang and stomped their feet and sang with their whole bodies. They had a beat, a powerful beat, a rhythm we held on to from slavery days, and their music was so strong and expressive it used to bring tears to my eyes. I believe the blues and jazz and even rock'n' roll stuff got their beat from the Sanctified Church (Boyer, 83-85).

Jackson was invited by an aunt to move to Chicago in 1927. She became a member of Greater Salem Baptist Church. She "accepted the invitation of the Johnson Brothers—Robert, Prince, and William—to join their singing group in 1929. The [Johnson] brothers," asserts Boyer "was the first organized gospel group in Chicago." Jackson's emotional outbursts in church were shocking to some members of the congregation (Boyer, 86).

Jackson became a Dorsey disciple in 1930—two years after her invitation to move to Chicago. She was more Pentecostal than Baptist in her singing style, and Dorsey liked to train his singers in his style. That didn't always work with Jackson. Dorsey says: "I tried to show Mahalia how to breathe and phrase, but she wouldn't listen. She said I was trying to make a stereotyped singer out of her. She may have been right" (Broughton, 53).

Nevertheless, Jackson joined Dorsey's team, became a revival singer, and joined Pilgrim's Gospel Chorus. She also sang for hospital and home visitation ministries. A member of the "University Radio Singers", the first radio singing group organized by Dorsey, Jackson traveled around the country singing with Dorsey (Kemp, 2011, 46) while also appearing annually at the National Baptist Convention. Her attempts to take formal voice lessons ended in failure. Her first gospel recording in 1937 didn't bring in much revenue.

In need of steady employment until her singing career was firmly established, Jackson studied at Madame C. J. Walker's famous beauty school and became an entrepreneur. She did hair during the week and performed singing engagements on the weekends. The noted singer and composer James Cleveland was her paper boy, and in a well-documented anecdote admits to standing outside her beauty shop just to hear her sing.

> I'd go over to her apartment on Indiana Avenue and
> leave her paper and then put my ear to the door to

try to hear her singing. If she wasn't at home, I'd go over to her beauty shop—she used to be a hairdresser you know—and just sit around there and listen to her hum songs while she was straightening hair (Carpenter, 2005, 87-88).

Jackson's fame as a gospel superstar was cemented when she sung at Carnegie Hall with the National Baptist Convention in 1950, an event which prompted huge revenues in her recording career. She appeared on the Ed Sullivan Show and landed a role in the movie "Imitation of Life." However, Jackson refused to pursue a secular singing career despite the acclaim and exposure she was receiving.

Jackson was also an important supporter of the Civil Rights Movement. She is revered for her rendition of the song "Move on Up a Little Higher." Dr. Martin Luther King, Jr., was very fond of her, so much so that she is depicted in the 2015 movie *Selma* as being the one he called during a low point when he needed to be lifted by his favorite song, "Precious Lord."

She sang "I Been 'Buked, and I Been Scorned" on August 28, 1963, climaxing the historic March on Washington, but she may best be remembered for singing Dorsey's masterpiece "Precious Lord, Take My Hand" at the funeral services for King in 1968 (Broughton, 55-56).

After her death on January 27, 1972, thousands mourned her in Chicago by viewing her body at her home church, The Greater Salem Baptist Church, and filling McCormick Place's 6,000-seat theater —the city's largest convention center's—where her funeral took place the following day. A second funeral took place in New Orleans, with a silent tribute and a funeral at the Rivergate Convention Center. A large statue of her is erected in New Orleans's famous Louis Armstrong Park. She was the posthumous recipient of a Grammy and has been honored with a U.S. postage stamp.

James Cleveland. James Cleveland, known familiarly as the "Crown Prince of Gospel Music" and the "King of Gospel Music," was also shepherded by Thomas Dorsey. Cleveland's grandmother was a member of Dorsey's gospel chorus, and he often accompanied her to choir rehearsals, where he learned the words of the songs taught during rehearsal and sang along with the choir. He soon became the unofficial "mascot" of the Pilgrim Gospel Chorus.

Dorsey wrote the song "All I Need Is Jesus" for young Cleveland, and he performed the song, his first solo, at the age of eight (Kemp, 70). He stood on a platform and sang it in a beautiful soprano voice during one of Pilgrim's Sunday morning services.

Cleveland was an integral part of NCGCC, leading the youth music ministry, until he left to form his own music organization The Gospel Music Workshop of America (GMWA) (Kemp, 2011). There, he became a mentor in his own right to the next group of gospel giants that included the late "Father of Contemporary Gospel," Andrae Crouch. Cleveland and Thurston Frazier published Crouch's first song "The Blood Shall Never Lose Its Power" (Kemp, 92).

The influence of Dorsey's organization, NCGCC is evident, both in the structure and practices of the GMWA. Most notably, the opening Sunday communion service at GMWA closely resembles the consecration service of NCGCC. Second Vice-President Bessie M. Palmer of the NCGCC remembers Cleveland frequently attending and performing at the convention throughout the years (Personal Interview, 2014).

Other Musicians Influenced by Dorsey

Thomas Dorsey trained a number of musicians throughout his years in the music ministry. Among them were singers Julia Mae Smith [Whitfield] and Marion [Purnell] Peebles. Both singers, along with

55

Willie Ruffin, were members of his group, The Celestial Trio. Peebles and Smith continued their ministry and service at Pilgrim Baptist Church and within the NCGCC, Whitfield working closely with Thomas Dorsey and Sallie Martin.

Julia Mae Smith. Julia Mae Smith (1918-1998) was born in Springfield, Ohio, the twelfth of thirteen children born to Thomas and Anna Eliza (Cunningham) Smith. Her father was a Sunday school superintendent, and her mother was the church musician at the Mount Zion Baptist Church of Springfield, Ohio. Brother Tommy Smith was a popular drummer and bandleader in Cincinnati, Ohio, and sister, Vivian Smith, was an original member of the Wings Over Jordan singing group.

Smith learned to play the piano from her mother and also studied under Ada House at Antioch College in Yellow Springs, Ohio. At age ten, she succeeded her mother as the church musician when she died. She met Thomas Dorsey and Sallie Martin when they came to Springfield to promote gospel music. After hearing her sing and play, they invited her to come to Chicago.

After arriving in Chicago in 1941, Smith accompanied Martin and toured with The Sallie Martin Singers. She joined Pilgrim in 1949 and became the pianist of the Gospel Chorus. She served as Professor Dorsey's assistant until 1992 and also as Pilgrim's Church Membership Secretary. Smith founded the group The Julia Smith Choralaires, served as directress of the Evangelical Choral Chapter and Gentlemen of Harmony, was organist and pianist for the A.R. Leak Funeral Homes, and the Financial Secretary for the NCGCC. She left a rich legacy in the lives of her daughter and granddaughter, who continue Levitical service in voice and instrument (Personal Interview, 2014).

Thomas A. Dorsey as Worship Leader

Old Testament writers speak of the use of singers, dancers, and musicians in Levitical worship duties in the Books of Chronicles and Nehemiah. The Psalms were also incorporated into religious worship, and they were sung by the Israelites during their yearly pilgrimages to Jerusalem, at their annual feasts, and during their sacred observances. Early Christians sang "spiritual songs and hymns" (Colossians 3:16), illustrating their importance in worship.

King David, the Lion of Judah, shepherd, poet, and warrior, however, retains the distinction as the chief worship leader of the Old Testament. Many of the Psalms are ascribed to him and were written for the Levitical worship leaders and the congregation. Some Psalms are ascribed to other Levitical musicians and to Moses, yet David is credited with establishing the institution of the Levitical temple service (1 Chronicles 6: 31-33; 9:33; 2 Chronicles 7:6; Ezra 3:10-11 [KJV]).

In the tradition of David, Thomas A. Dorsey filled the role of what is today a "worship leader." He served for many years (from 1932 to the 1980s) as the musical director for the historic Pilgrim Baptist Church on Chicago's South Side, and is responsible to a considerable degree for the church's designation as an historical landmark. Dr. Dorsey wasn't able to attend church regularly after his health began to fail. There were occasions, however, when he would still direct.

Pastor Deborah Smith recalled a musical she attended at Pilgrim with her husband, Director Joseph Smith during Dorsey's waning years: "He was whistling like a bird" [to the lyrics of the song]. She later told her husband that "whistling is an outside thing, unless you're Dr. Dorsey. He's the only one who can whistle in the house" (Personal Interview, 2014).

In the lyrics he composed for praise and worship—poems and songs in the tradition of David—Dorsey wrote about the goodness of God and of the assurances of His son Jesus the Christ. Just as in Old Testament Levitical worship services, Dorsey's songs were written for twentieth-century individual and corporate worship services.

The parallels between the songs Dorsey wrote and the praise poetry of the Psalms are both evident and striking—works that were the centerpieces of worship used by the Levites, who directed, composed, taught and led the Hebrew people in worship and praise. Although Dorsey was not duly recognized as a minister of the preached gospel until the 1960s, his standing and legacy as a Levite in the praise and worship services of the African American people for whom he wrote his gospels songs is assured. This legacy is perpetuated through the convention associated with his name.

Dorsey's Parallels with King David

Dorsey's biographer, Ruth Smith, called to mind Dorsey's parallels with King David in the former's battle to establish the sacredness of the gospel genre in a hostile environment that sought to undermine it and David's battle with the Old Testament kings. David fought kings. Dorsey fought organized religion. Smith also gives this additional depiction of Dorsey's character and personality. His regal carriage and strong belief system are reminiscent of qualities of David.

> ...affable, a strong perfectionist, [strict] work ethic; tacit but with a sense of humor, not egotistical; Christian-like in his demeanor, [and] believes in his convictions, liberal in sharing, conservative in activities, lives in simple surroundings but walks regally. Dorsey loves the out-of-doors, swimming, boating, fishing and sports (Smith, 25-26).

Dorsey's strong work ethic is evidenced by his involvement in different enterprises: He was a founder and president of the first organization dedicated to gospel music; a singer; a music publisher; a copywriter; a poet; a director; a teacher; a gospel musician; a prolific gospel composer (see Appendix VI for a list of the many sacred songs he wrote); and until 1940, a secular musician.

There are many resources that supply information about Dorsey's secular and sacred achievements, but few speak to his poetry and teaching style. He taught, sung, spoke, played, and directed choirs and choruses wherever he travelled. He provided explanations in some of his songbooks of the inspiration he received [from God] for the lyrics to the songs. Elder William Fuqua relates one such workshop experience in Columbus, Georgia, wherein Dorsey's attributes as a modern-day Levite were on full display:

> He taught "The Lord Will Make a Way Somehow" and "Take My Hand, Precious Lord." He wanted his songs sung exactly like he wrote them....He also had his poems; books on choir decorum; books on ways to direct a choir; and books on the proper ways to conduct meetings. That was my first workshop experience with Thomas Dorsey. I never did forget it (Personal Interview, 2014).

Marion Peebles distinguishes between how Dorsey taught for instruction in rehearsal and what he expected during actual performances. She also noted that he never directed from music in performances.

> We always had music to rehearse, but when we get up [Mr. Dorsey would say] "put that book down"....the senior choirs, they would put their portfolios—their folders

with the music—and they sang from the music. We did not. We sang from the music in rehearsals (Jackson, 2004, 62).

In 1945, Dorsey published the book of poems *Dorsey's Poem Book for All Occasions*. The paraphrased preface introduced them as poems for every occasion to fulfill a need in homes, churches, societies, lodges, and schools; to uplift hearts, and give the world a poem. They convey a deep spiritual meaning and message to help save souls and to encourage and inspire contemporary writers. Edith Tillotson, in highlighting Dorsey's Levitical attribute as a poet, included in her work a poem that he wrote in 1945, "Negro Music":

> Sweet songs that come oft from a troubled heart—sad
> songs that oppression brings—Songs that once heard
> are ne'er forgot
> Are the songs that the Negro sings.
> Music that comes from a soul sincere
> And ascends to God above.
> Music as only time can teach,
> Is the music a Negro loves,
> In a voice of anguish and longing—
> Ere Liberty's flag unfurled.
> In words, broken with fervent prayer
> Is the Negro's song to the world.
> Sad music of longing sweet music of hope—
> And songs of far Jordan's Roll,
> Tunes of tears and tunes of smiles,
> Are the chants of a Negro's soul.

Chapter Four:

The National Convention of Gospel Choirs and Choruses

"Let the Word of Christ dwell in you richly in all wisdom: teaching and admonishing one another in psalms and hymns and spiritual songs, singing with grace in your hearts to the Lord (Colossians 3:16, KJV).

Thomas A. Dorsey's reputation as a modern-day prophet can probably be best established by his foresight in recognizing the significance of an emerging sacred music idiom, the gospel song, and in devoting his energies to the promotion and instruction of singers in its proper delivery. The means by which he was able to accomplish these goals was the establishment of the first national organization to serve the needs of gospel singers: The National Convention of Gospel Choirs and Choruses. The organization went a long way to legitimizing gospel music as a sacred musical genre in the United States and beyond. The convention is dedicated not only to preserving Dorsey's music and legacy, but also to training youth for service in church music and as worship leaders, much as the rules and regulations issued in the Books of Leviticus and Numbers did for the Levites.

The first gospel choral union was organized August 17, 1932. Dorsey invited two well-known and respected choir directors to a meeting to organize a city-wide gospel chorus. They were Magnolia

Lewis Butts, directress of the W.D. Cook Gospel Choir of the Metropolitan Community Church, and Professor Theodore R. Frye, director
of the Ebenezer Gospel Chorus of the Ebenezer Missionary Baptist
Church. The meeting took place at Butts's church. At the time, there
were very few women directresses. That position was reserved for
men. Thomas Dorsey was among the first to include women in this
organization.

The Widespread Acceptance of the NCGCC

The original name of the convention was the National Convention of
Gospel Choirs, Choruses and Smaller Musical Groups, Inc., and it grew
from six to twenty groups within one year. This widespread acceptance
led to the organization of the national convention, which became The
National Convention of Gospel Choirs and Choruses (NCGCC). The
first convention was held at Pilgrim Baptist Church in Chicago from
August 30, 1933 to September 1, 1933. Appendix III shows the time-
line of succeeding conventions from 1933 to 2014.

Edith Tillotson (1976) characterizes the importance of the sung
gospel in this quote: "Gospel is just another part of the musical tree,
another added branch in America's history. What was the purpose of
man writing music in that day? History documents the impact of
Dorsey's songs to black people in the 1930s and 1940s."

The songs fed the souls of those who sang them, and they im-
parted courage and inspiration to those who heard their messages.
Dorsey's songs comforted people through trials and heartaches, en-
couraging them to hold on and look to heaven for strength. They were,
in Heilbut's, words "good news and bad times" (Walker, 127).

Dorsey spoke from personal experience. The "Precious Lord"
story is well known. The death of his first wife Nettie and day-old son
caused a spiritual crisis. It caused Thomas to become bitter with God.

Faith results from believing in something and someone you can't see with the physical eye. Strength is gained through times of pain and hardship. Dorsey relied on God to sustain and carry him through these times of personal crisis. Rev. Jeremiah A. Wright, Jr., affirmed this truth in the PBS Documentary, "We've Come This Far by Faith": Part 3:

> Persons of deep faith are not exempt from crisis; they are not exempt from hardship, and they are not exempt from disappointment. They are not exempt from getting knocked down by life and by circumstances, and, at those times when you are knocked down, you can't make it on your own, not on your own strength; you need a strength that is not your own (Transcript, 13).

An "Unsuitable" Prophet

Dorsey may not have been considered by some pastors as a suitable prophet or traveling evangelist, but he carried his message throughout the country through his music and through his organization that promoted it. Samuel's words come to mind, which remind people who judge that only man looks at the outward appearances: "for the Lord seeth not as man seeth; for man looketh on the outward appearance, but the Lord looketh on the heart" (1 Samuel 16:7b) [KJV]).

Proverbs 21:2 shows God's true concern. "Every way of a man is right in his own eyes: but the Lord pondereth the hearts" (KJV). Although the temporal shepherds, the various pastors of churches, could not see what God had done within Dorsey's heart, Jesus, the chief shepherd knew because God was the "author and finisher" of Dorsey's faith. God knew the assignment He had placed on Dorsey's life.

Thomas Dorsey had strict rules for those who wanted to become members of NCGCC. First, they had to belong to a church; secondly, they had to provide written permission from their pastors that they were in good standing at their local church. Lastly, they couldn't participate in any NCGCC functions that interfered with planned activities at their home church. Dorsey stressed that discipleship and service to their individual churches was of the upmost importance as well as their primary duty.

Edith J. Tillotson compiled a collection of articles, pictures, and programs of the NCGCC from the years 1932 to 1975 in the book *Gospel Born: A Pictorial and Poetic History of the National Convention of Gospel Choirs and Choruses* (1976). The book was assembled as a scholarship fundraiser for the youth department of the convention. A number of people collaborated on the book. Among them were Gloria C. Wright, Grace Bonner, Mary Wilks, John Thomas, Beverly McGinnis, Helen Minor, Murdie Hughes, Loda Byrd, and Elizabeth McIntosh. It names Sallie Martin, Magnolia Butts, and Theodore Frye as co-founders of the convention. Marion M. Pairs and Henry J. Carruthers are also named with the original organizers. I.J. Johnson, Artelia Hutchins, Theo Brown, and H.J. Carruthers were brought in by Sallie Martin. Artelia Hutchins is the person who instituted the educational classes, which are now an integral component of each convention.

The Goals of the NCGCC's Founders

The founders of the convention wanted to clarify their goals and to distinguish the unique purpose and sound of the sacred genre of gospel music. This was to refute the claims of churches regarding its style and its similarity to secular music. The Preamble of the NCGCC sets forth the organization's goals:

...in order to perpetuate the beautiful Spirituals that were the spontaneous outbursts of the Negro's heart in the dark days of slavery and which have proven themselves to be such a priceless contribution to American civilization; to promote and appreciate the Gospel Songs of this day and time, which touch the hearts of men; to prepare singers to carry the Gospel in song in an intelligent manner and to make it clear that there is a vast difference between the songs that are inspired by our Heavenly Father and the common "jazz" music so prevalent today, we herewith organize this National Convention.

(Article Section 1, National Convention of Gospel Choirs and Choruses, By-laws and Constitution).

Key Leaders of the NCGCC

Early convention leaders of the NCGCC included Kenneth Morris, Theodore R. Frye, Dr. A.W. Womack, and J.B. Green. As articulated in its bylaws and constitution, this convention was designed to "better equip Christian singers, instrumentalists, educators, and leaders to become better prepared gospel ambassadors and spiritually motivated to live the message of the gospel song."

As the convention grew, departments, choral unions, chapters, and choirs were added. Pastors who became a part of the convention were designated advisory board members. In 1933, Dorsey created the *Gospel Singers' News*, the first publication of its kind. The monthly publication informed the members of NCGCC about gospel news and gospel singers and offered advice, hints, and printed articles about gospel music. It also gave members highlights of board meetings (Smith, 40).

The powerful singing evangelist, Mother Willie Mae Ford Smith—the same woman who had purportedly "wrecked" the National Baptist Convention with Dorsey's song in the 1930s—established a soloist's bureau. Originally established as the "Soloists' Council," the bureau became known as the Soloist Bureau in 1944. Its mission was to foster soloists who come with ambitions to sing, as well as to foster convention soloists. Well-known leaders of the bureau included Rosa Nell Elmore and Magnolia Butts.

Just as Dorsey trained soloists to be his disciples in presenting his songs, he had an inner circle of people whose efforts led to the growth of the NCGCC as a national organization. Willie Mae Ford Smith, Professor Theodore Frye, and Magnolia Lewis Butts were part of that circle. The story of NCGCC was depicted powerfully in the documentary "Say Amen Somebody (1983)." The 2001 PBS retelling of that story shows the hard work and dedication of those who made the organization a place that trained singers to minister for the Lord through their music.

Willie Mae Ford Smith. Willie Mae Ford Smith (1904-1994) sang gospel music when it was not popular to do so. She used it to evangelize and preach the word in her outreach throughout the city and wherever she was invited. Smith was the first black to sing gospel music at Kiel Auditorium in St. Louis and to take gospel to the world—to preach it everywhere. Her ministry began in April, 1944 at the True Light Baptist Church. Her contributions included conducting more than 1,000 revivals, teaching soloists, and doing mission work as God saw fit. She told them that gospel music must be understood and enunciated.

Although she had no musical credentials, she was gifted by God to spread the gospel in song and to evangelize everywhere she went. She cautioned singers not to sing gospel for money or

Grammy nominations, but for the glory of God. In her concluding comments for the documentary, she said "gospel singing is a different singing when you're anointed by God—that's what you're striving for." No other medium conveys the power, the presence, and the authority, the magnificence of a God who loves us always, in spite of what we have done or may do. No other ministry sings of a God who forgives and gives another chance.

Theodore R. Frye. Theodore R. Frye (1899-1963) was born in Fayette, Mississippi. He had served as a soloist and choir director before migrating to Chicago in 1927. He met Dorsey, who became his pianist and accompanied him when he had singing engagements. They became close friends and worked together for many years. Like Dorsey, Frye, a composer, worked with Roberta Martin and Mahalia Jackson. He became a co-founder of the National Baptist Music Convention in 1948. He also worked with Thomas Dorsey and Lilian Bowles in their publishing businesses, later opening his own in 1948 (Boyer, 64-65).

As a co-founder of the NCGCC, Frye instituted the junior department training school of the convention for the youth division, which was organized in 1939. He appointed supervisors to portray the spiritual goals needed for the youth. The youth performed their songs on Friday night. The first youth supervisor in 1933 was Roberta Martin. The department has expanded, and is now known as the Youth and Young Adult Department. James Cleveland was once their musical director. The duties of a youth supervisor are addressed in Section 10 of the convention's by-laws.

> ...to organize, train, foster, instruct the children on
> how to carry on the business of their organizations.
> A day was also designated at each convention for the
> youth to lead in many capacities...to recruit youth;
> stimulate an appreciation for the music of the negro

composer, provide wholesome recreation for their leisure hours; maintain an operating expense fund; provide chaperones for all youth activities; provide adequate counseling service for all youth problems; support the parent body and the rules/guidelines.

(National Convention of Gospel Choirs and Choruses, By-laws and Constitution)

Youth Supervisors. Other youth supervisors were Cassie Wright, Mary Maddox, Cornelia Moss, Mary L. Wright, Catherine Burrell, Alvina Montgomery, Carol E. Hayes, and Beatrice Brown. Their responsibilities were those detailed in the bylaws and constitution. The last Sunday in June was set aside as the day to raise funds for the various scholarship departments in the youth and adult departments. The winners were able to submit their applications and plan accordingly for future educational needs in the fall. The supervisors had twenty-four hour responsibility for the youth during the convention. Youth in the host cities, however, were invited to participate in activities that were scheduled during the day.

Magnolia Lewis Butts. Magnolia Lewis Butts (1880-1949) was gifted in music ministry. As a soloist, she is best remembered for her 1942 composition "Let It Breathe on Me." Boyer remarks on its continued use for altar call and meditation into the 1990s (Boyer, 65).

Magnolia Butts was a powerful force at the convention. She nominated Dorsey for president, led the first bylaws committee, served as a mediator, and compiled the first minutes. She offered resolutions for forming the scholarship department, interpreted laws for governance, printed and designed credential forms for choirs and choruses, and recommended the institution of an artists' night (Tillotson, 1976). Her chief contribution however, was the consecration and dedication service, which, to many, is the highlight of the convention.

The Consecration Service, the Highlight of the Convention

The consecration service is held on Monday morning. On Sunday night, a dedicated group of ministers, evangelists, singers, and officers meet to prepare the room for the service. After a short devotional period, chairs and tables are set up for the service. The sheets and table coverings are carried from convention to convention. They are cleaned and shipped to arrive in time at the next convention site. The person in charge of the consecration is in charge of the consecration chest.

The annual journey of the consecration chest, has parallels to that Levitical service performed for The Tent of Meeting (which served as their sanctuary), and was put up and taken down, much as when the children of Israel moved from place to place. The descendants of Levi were given specific duties in the service of the Lord for worship. Moses recorded this commandment from God concerning his charge to the sons of Aaron—the family designated to serve as priests for the children of Israel: "...behold, I have taken your brethren the Levites from among the children of Israel: to you they are given as a gift for the Lord, to do the service of the tabernacle of the congregation" Numbers 18:6 (KJV).

After a devotional period, prayers, songs, and instrumental music on keyboard continue while the room is prepared for the consecration service. Chairs in the first two rows are draped with white sheets and pinned. The pulpit chairs are also covered, while the pulpit itself is draped in white with two red stripes. Choir pews are covered until all consecration material has been used. The table of consecration, in the center of the room, is adorned with a gold and white garment. This table covering is a Levitical symbol passed down from consecration leader to consecration leader. The tradition began when Magnolia Butts passed the garment to Fannie Foster in 1942. In turn, Fannie Foster gave it to Geneva Gentry, who replaced her in 1976. Geneva Gentry (1912-2013), was the wife of Joshua Gentry (1912-1990), who served as first, second, and third vice presidents for NCGCC, and also is the mother of the current president, Dr. Marabeth Gentry. Gentry passed the mantle on to Overseer Loreta Garrett when she was no longer able to attend the annual convention.

The preparation ends with prayer, scripture, and a prophetic word. The next day, all assemble for the consecration service, which includes the ministerial staff's anointing, individually, all who are present. This service makes a specific impact on those attending, as it places the participants in a sacred space. Prayers and prophecies are offered up for those who are present, and petitions for their health and their families are likewise lifted up. As they leave with smiles and tears, delegates often remark that the service carries them throughout the year. Feeling loved, appreciated, and replenished with a sense of commitment to the ministry of music, they eagerly anticipate the next year when they can once again rededicate their lives to serving others through song.

The Leading Gospel Soloists and Groups of the NCGCC: 1930s-1960s

Among the leading convention soloists and groups were Mahalia Jackson, Grace L. Bonner, Frankie Fambro Carrington, Robert Anderson, The Mighty Clouds of Joy; Delois Barrett, Clara Ward, and James Cleveland. C. Hatchet and Ruth Sloan Taylor were national accompanists for the singers. Section 8 of the constitution defined the role of the accompanist in these words: "[the] duty of the accompanist shall be to furnish instrumental music for the sessions; to accompany the soloists on the various programs, unless otherwise provided for." The convention's composers included Roberta Martin, Sallie Martin, Professor A. B. Wendom, and C.E. Pringle (Tillotson).

The NCGCC Seeks to Establish a Home for Gospel Singers

Thomas Dorsey's vision was to purchase a home in Chicago at a modest price for itinerant gospel singers. He was able to purchase this home in 1935 and named it "Gospel Singers' Rest." It housed a music department to teach singing, playing, and directing. Its intended purpose was to provide housing for gospel singers (Smith, 1935). Unfortunately, the venture was short-lived.

Subsequently, the NCGCC bought a building to continue Dorsey's vision to create a Gospel Singers School of Music and Associate Artists. He presented the idea to the convention in 1942, and it was adopted. By 1945, a building was purchased for that purpose at 4048 S. Lake Park in Chicago, which became the Gospel Singers School and Home. The convention took possession of the building in 1948 and opened the dormitories to singers from all over the country. A school opened in October 1949 for out-or-town students. Private and class instruction were offered. The building was available to rent for teas, recitals, banquets, rehearsals, weddings, and club meetings (Tillotson, 45).

Like Dorsey, Sallie Martin also had a dream to establish a permanent complex in Chicago that would carry on the vision of gospel music begun by the pioneering work of Dorsey and herself. To that end, she took out a $1,200,000 loan to build a plaza dedicated to gospel music on Chicago's South Side. The plaza fronted a twenty-six room mansion at 4048 Lake Park Avenue and was dedicated in April 1971, fulfilling Martin's dream for a memorial to house the history of gospel music in Chicago. The dream did not last, as the National Convention was unable to keep up the payments and maintenance of the building.

The Continuing Vision

The NCGCC has continued the vision of its founders into the twenty-first century. Bishop Kenneth Moales, who succeeded Thomas Dorsey, preserved the Dorsey legacy with an annual founder's service, while strengthening and broadening existing departments. The Artelia Hutchins Training Institute, founded in 1950 by Artelia W. Hutchins, who at one time also served as First Vice President of NCGCC, was first simply called the "Leadership School." (She, along with Professor Dorsey, wrote the well-known song used as a church benediction and still is found in many hymnals: "God Be With You"). This educational component offers training and historical data that relates to music education, church worship practices, and the convention's history.

Dr. Ulysses Moye II, Dean of the AHTI and Third Vice President, coordinates the program of studies for the annual conventions. The institute offers college continuing education credit for successful completion of a three-year certification process from a newly established partnership with the Washington, D.C. Theological Seminary.

The history of NCGCC is disseminated in an on-going class which, in 1998, produced its first oral history CD with interviews from key figures who had been a part of the organization throughout the years.

The Pastoral Alliance Department, under the leadership of Pastor Albert L. Morgan, Fifth Vice President, conducts seminars where musicians and pastors interact while solving problems and addressing issues related to the roles of church leadership and music ministry.

Keeble Carries the Torch

In the 1990s, the Rev. Dr. Stanley Keeble, President of the Chicago Gospel Heritage Museum, and a former Chicago high school English teacher, attempted to resurrect the vision to establish a permanent memorial to the pioneering gospel artists who made Chicago the "mecca of gospel music." God said to him: "I want you to put together a gospel museum," he relates (Interview, Kemp, Issue, 20). To date, however, no permanent building in Chicago has been created as a gospel music haven, and no permanent physical building exists in Chicago where lovers of gospel music and students of its ministry can visit.

Dr. Keeble, an anointed singer, director, and musician has accompanied Bessie Griffin, Jessy Dixon, and Inez Andrews and has served as pianist, organist, and director for the Radio Choir of Fellowship Baptist Church, under the leadership of Rev. Dr. Clay Evans in Chicago. His gospel music contributions were honored by Chicago HistoryMakers in 2006; he participated in a Mahalia Jackson interview for a BBC documentary [London 2012], and is a recipient of many awards for gospel music, including the Gospel Supreme (2008) and the Living Legend GMAC Award (2010). He remarked poignantly that today's students [he'd taught] didn't even know the legacy of Thomas Dorsey (Interview: issuu.com).

While the DuSable Museum of African American History has featured an exhibit on gospel music during Black History Month, and some churches maintain their own archival collections, there exists no central location in Chicago today to house this rich heritage. The present collection of artifacts for these archives for the gospel pioneers named "The Magnificent Eight" is housed with Dr. Keeble. The "Magnificent Eight," as they were called, began with Dr. Thomas A. Dorsey and includes as members the gospel luminaries Thomas Dorsey, Sallie Martin, Theodore Frye, Roberta Martin, Mahalia Jackson, James Cleveland, Milton Brunson, and Roebuck "Pop" Staples.

Dorsey's Honors and Awards

Thomas Dorsey lived long enough to enjoy the many honors and awards that were bestowed upon him for his contributions to black sacred music. He was honored extensively throughout the 1980s, a period during which he continued to perform and produce albums. He also participated in music seminars throughout the country and particularly enjoyed fielding and answering questions about gospel music. He left his gospel archives to Fisk University during this time.

Dorsey was ecumenical in the best sense of the word, and engaged with any and all who believed in God, no matter what a person's denomination happened to be. He was a generous man, who helped to raise money for African children through the Women's Auxiliary of the Kingdom of God (an extension of the Original African Hebrew Israelite Nation of Jerusalem). He appeared annually on programs in Holiness and Spiritual churches and districts.

The Death of Thomas A. Dorsey

Thomas A. Dorsey was remembered warmly after his death at home in Chicago on January 23, 1993. He was mourned by hundreds at his funeral services, which were held at Pilgrim Baptist Church, where he had overseen the musical selections for the church's gospel choir for more than 60 years, and where he had arranged the music for the choir, soloists, and choral groups. He was recognized for the many "firsts" that marked the many awards and accomplishments that were his legacy.

74

The Gospel Fest held annually in Chicago, Illinois, began as the "Dorsey Gospel Fest" in the 1980s under the leadership of the late Mayor Jane M. Byrne. The name was changed two years later to the "Chicago Gospel Fest." The festival continues to honor the heritage of the Bronzeville community in Chicago, which is the birthplace and the home of gospel music. In acknowledgment of Thomas Dorsey's singular role in cementing Chicago's title as the undisputed home of gospel music, his signature song "Precious Lord" stands next to the hymn "Amazing Grace" as one of the most revered sacred songs ever written.

The Push for a Black Heritage U.S. Postage Stamp

The efforts of supporters of Thomas Dorsey to have his legacy commemorated with a Black Heritage U.S. postage stamp have proven unsuccessful as this book goes to print. The denial of this recognition to Dorsey is based on the policy of the U.S. Postal Service not to issue stamps or stationery items to honor religious institutions or individuals whose principal achievements are associated with religious undertakings or beliefs.

This refusal to accord Dorsey such an honor, in the opinion of this author and that of many others, is particularly surprising, given the fact that singers and performers whom Dorsey mentored and influenced have had commemorative stamps issued to honor their achievements. As cases in point, Gertrude "Ma" Rainey, Roberta Martin, Mahalia Jackson, Clara Ward, and Sister Rosetta [Tharpe] have had the distinction of a postage stamp issued in their honor. Few would doubt that, as gospel singers, Martin, Jackson, and Ward are associated with religious undertakings. Indeed, all except Ma Rainey were affiliated with church worship, and all of the aforementioned singers were active in the NCGCC at different times. Mahalia Jackson, in particular, was a regular soloist for the National Baptist Convention. Sister Rosetta Tharpe, like Dorsey, was also well known for both sacred and secular music.

Thomas Dorsey, as the acknowledged "Father of Gospel Music" would, in the eyes of many, be eminently worthy of a commemorative stamp if he were judged by the same criteria as other—and lesser—accomplished recipients of the honor. Gospel music in and of itself is music rendered to God. Gospel singers sing music rendered unto God. What is the difference between gospel songs sung and composed by Roberta Martin, Clara Ward, and Mahalia Jackson and those sung by Thomas Dorsey? His best known composition, "Precious Lord" is recognized and loved throughout the world and is sung in churches, chapels, cathedrals, and concert halls, yet he has not been honored with a Black Heritage stamp. This author, as well as Dorsey's legion of admirers, believes that it is high time that the oversight be rectified.

Chapter Five:

Interviews with Dorsey's Admirers and Contemporaries

The author interviewed several contemporaries and admirers of Thomas A. Dorsey and recorded their recollections and fond memories of the acknowledged "Father of Gospel Music." The interviewees shared their impressions of the man, their experiences with the organization he founded, The National Convention of Gospel Choirs and Choruses, and their assessment of the impact that he had on the gospel music genre as a form of sacred music. They also expressed their concerns about the preservation of his legacy at a time when the identity of gospel music is under siege by the secularization of its message for commercial profit. Interviewees include pastors of churches, ministers of music, singers, choir directors, musicians mentored in the gospel tradition, a niece of Thomas Dorsey, songwriters, as well as officers and members of the NCGCC. The author expresses deep gratitude to them for sharing so generously their knowledge, experiences, insights, and perspectives on the gospel music genre and its challenges in conveying the Word of God through song in the twenty-first century and beyond.

Almond Dawson, Jr.

(Personal Interview, July, 2014)

Almond Dawson, Jr., is a well-known musician and director. He served as guest musician for the Second District Chorus—COGIC—

for more than twenty years. He also was the pianist and arranger for The Inspirational Singers, a Chicago gospel group who sang in many venues and was featured on "Jubilee Showcase" with Sid Ordower. Dawson is active in many musical organizations throughout the city of Chicago and across the nation. He shared his recollections of Thomas Dorsey with the author in an interview.

AD: I played for Professor Dorsey in Milwaukee, Wisconsin. I was the guest pianist, and he was the guest soloist. Thelma Gould was a member of the Church of the Living God Temple 78. She served as Director of the Second District Chorus.

KK: Who made up the Second District Chorus?

AD: Members were from the States of Illinois, Wisconsin, and Missouri. The Second District Council met in Milwaukee, the one year that I served as guest musician. It was in late spring.

KK: That's when you accompanied Thomas Dorsey?

AD: Yes. Mr. Dorsey came in. He was wearing a very heavy coat. He sat down, all hunched over. They told him I was the guest musician. He asked me: "Do you know how to play "Precious Lord," young man?" I said, "Yes, Professor Dorsey. I am a member of Monumental Baptist Church." It was located at 729 E. Oakwood Blvd. The Dorsey home was [down the street] at 755 E. Oakwood.

KK: Was that building [Dorsey's home] a historical site?

78

AD: The building has been torn down. It was never made a historic site, perhaps because it needed extensive repairs. No one did anything to preserve it or to mark the location as the former home of Professor Dorsey.

KK: The home in which he resided until his death, however, at 7921 S. Indiana, Chicago, Illinois, acknowledges him with a marker on the front lawn.

AD: When Professor Dorsey was called to sing, his appearance and demeanor changed. He threw off the coat and walked very briskly. When he directed, he held his fingers up like a fist. He looked at me and began singing "Precious Lord." He directed me as he sang, telling me when to play louder for more emphasis...."

KK: Was that your only meeting with him?

AD: I saw him on many occasions after that. We were not personal friends, but Mr. Dorsey always acknowledged me and remembered that connection.

Elder William Fuqua
(Personal Interview, August, 2014)

Elder William R. Fuqua is a well-known gospel historian. He is a pianist, organist, and composer. In the early 2000s, he contributed his vast gospel music collection to the library of the Gospel Music Workshop of America, Inc. Elder Fuqua has played for churches around the country and lectures on gospel music history. His contributions to the author's first publication *Make a Joyful Noise: A Brief History of Gospel Music Ministry in America* were invaluable. He recounts his first personal encounter with the teaching of Professor Dorsey in this interview.

KK: What is your personal recollection of Thomas Dorsey?

WF: I remember him from a workshop I attended in Columbus, Georgia, related to the Phenix City Choral Union, which is across the Chattahoochee River that divides Alabama and Georgia. It's across the bridge from Columbus.

KK: What made this such a memorable experience?

WF: I was seventeen years old in 1953 and living in Columbus. I took a Checker Cab to the Metropolitan Baptist Church on Fifth Avenue pastored by the late Rev. Cloud. This section of Columbus was called East Highland. I slammed my right thumb in the car door of the cab. I went into the service anyway because it was numb. The next morning, my Momma had to take me to the doctor. He put a metal brace on the thumb, which has never been the same since that incident.

KK: You remember very specific details about that event.

WF: Yes. The church was near the then Clafton Elementary School and the Central of Georgia railroad tracks that went to Atlanta. At that time, Metropolitan was one of the largest black churches in Columbus. Thomas Dorsey and Sallie Martin held a workshop there. It was on a Friday evening. They began to

80

teach at 8:00 P.M. Each took different sections in the church while they taught the individual parts to those in attendance.

KK: Then they team-tagged in their workshop?

WF: Musicians from all the local churches were invited and were in attendance, including [those from] Phenix City.

KK: How many people were there?

WF: I was a boy, but it seemed to me like it was eighty to one hundred people. It was a wide church, and they sat where the congregation would sit. Rev. Willie Smith was the president of the Phenix City/Columbus Choral Union. I think it was formed from that visit. The late Rev. Willie Smith from the Friendship Baptist Church on Sixth Avenue was the minister of music. He later became the pastor of Friendship, the church where Ma Rainey was a member. Ma Rainey was a blues singer, one of the best at that time. Thomas Dorsey was her pianist.

KK: Rev. Smith was instrumental in the Dorsey convention?

WF: Mrs. Willie Pearl Huff Rae was the organizer of the Sweet Chariot Gospel Singers. "Blind" Emory Jones was the pianist. They sang every Sunday morning on radio station WRBL in Columbus. Mrs. Rae and Rev. Smith were pioneers in the Thomas Dorsey Convention. They taught Dorsey's songs throughout the Georgia and Alabama area.

KK: What songs did he teach?

WF: He taught "The Lord Will Make a Way Somehow" and "Take My Hand, Precious Lord." He [Dorsey] wanted his songs sung exactly like he wrote them. He played on an upright piano.

KK: How did you know that he wanted his songs sung just like he wrote them?

WF: Because he said so. He was very finicky like that. In his buckle grip he had music for sale. The sheet music was called a ballot. He would sell them for ten and fifteen cents. He also had his poems, books on choir decorum, books on ways to direct a choir, and books on the proper ways to conduct meetings. That was my first workshop experience with Thomas Dorsey. I never did forget it. Mr. Dorsey was a teacher who wanted things to be done right.

Shirley Marchman

(Personal Interview, June, 2014)

Shirley Marchman is President of the Dorsey Birthplace Choir and a councilwoman for Villa Rica, Georgia. Shirley Marchman, a singer herself, also from a Levitical family, is co-chair for the Thomas Dorsey Fest. Councilwoman Marchman is involved in the youth, Sunday school, and musical ministries of her church—Mt. Prospect Baptist Church—the original church of the Dorsey family. Marchman said that growing up [in Villa Rica], they really didn't know who Thomas Dorsey was or that they were singing many of his songs. In later years, Villa Ricans learned about their rich legacy. The idea to commemorate his legacy happened after his death. Marchman is proud of the fact that Villa Rica is the only place that has the distinction of being the home of the Thomas Dorsey Birthplace Choir.

KK: How did the Thomas Dorsey Fest begin?

SM: Evan Wilson of Villa Rica talked to the mayor, Teddy Lee. Mr. Wilson said we needed to do something to keep Dr. Dorsey's memory alive, since he was born in Villa Rica. Mayor Lee told him to talk to me. We met at a restaurant called "The Mansion." We pondered what to do to keep his memory alive. I said "Why don't we start a choir, since he was about music?"

        I told him that I had cousins in music ministry: a singer, a director, and a musician. We sent out letters to the surrounding counties and areas inviting people to join the choir. After that, we formed the executive board with Evan Wilson as executive director until he moved away. Now we don't have an executive director.

KK: Who makes up the present board?

SM: Eric Ayers is the president, I am the secretary, and Rusty Dean is the treasurer. The other board members are Bernice Brooks, Darfus Dallas, Barbara Daniell, James Potts, Jeff Reese, Elizabeth Taylor, and Alfred Wilson.

KK: When did you become a part of the National Convention of Gospel Choirs and Choruses, the organization founded by Dr. Dorsey?

SM: Dorothy Grant, the national organizer, came from NCGCC to bring us into the convention. We were inducted on April 9, 1995. I have been the president since that time.

KK: Do you have a list of the founding members?

SM: We've had some of our staunch members to pass away. My mother and others.... the Lord has called them home, but we're still going on. The founding members that have passed are Ada Bailey; Ellena McCain—my mother; Charlie Styles, Jr.; Ernestine Styles; Verlyn Styles; A.D. Moore; and Mary Mitchell.

KK: How do people become a part of this choir?

SM: It's open to all people of all races....We sing without music....

KK: What would you do to share this festival with even more people?

SM   If [only] we could figure out a way to bring more gospel artists here....Eric usually gets our gospel guests to come in. You hear them on the radio talking about how Dr. Dorsey got them started.... Many people say they did this or that with Dr. Dorsey, but when you ask them to come, they come up with some astronomical amount of money. Can't you give something back if he means that much to you? We've been blessed, however, to have wonderful sponsors from this community and the surrounding area. It doesn't cost anything for the audience to come and be a part of it [the fest].

Dr. Dorsey was both gospel and blues….We have connections with different people… on the gospel and blues sides….

KK: The fest is very well attended.

SM: People are pleased…they really enjoy it. Twenty years is a long time, and, [yet] it is not a long time. I think [that] with the consistency, people are seeing that we're not just some little "fly by night" organization. They see how we have continued to not let it fall by the wayside. By the grace of God we have been successful to keep it going for twenty years. That's really a milestone. God is good. God is still good.

KK: Your current mayor spoke at the fest Saturday [June 28, 2014].

SM: The current mayor Jay Collins is very much involved with the fest. As a matter of fact, while attending a meeting at the state capitol a few weeks ago, he was promoting Dorsey. That's a good thing [his input]…and I, as a member of the city council, have good cooperation from the council. They see that we're about business, too. We do have two or three different festivals during the year. This is one of the main ones.

KK: So Villa Rica has included the Thomas Dorsey Festival as one of its major festivals?

SM: Yes. Yes, they have. We have banners that we put out on the street—you know they're expensive. They were donated. The city recreation department does that every year. The t-shirts are donated by Tanner Hospital. There are four Tanner

Hospitals.... Loy Howard, CEO of Tanner Hospitals, invited us to come and be a part of the celebration when they built the new hospital. He told me that he wanted to sponsor the t-shirts and has done the t-shirts for the last five years. That has been a blessing. We are happy to put their name on the back of the shirts. We send a thank-you letter, a program, and a t-shirt each year to Tanner and our other sponsors. That's one way we show our appreciation to them for all they do to make this festival a success.

KK: Who has come down to Villa Rica to learn more about your efforts?

SM: We've done a lot with the colleges and universities here....A men's choir—I think they were from Germany—came through, and we sang on a program with them at the University of West Georgia in Carrolton.

KK: Didn't I hear you say that the Smithsonian Institute had been down to visit and tape the choir in Villa Rica when you spoke at the Douglas County Center Poet's Afternoon Program last year?

SM: The Smithsonian sponsored a program for Black History Month in February 2013. It was called "Celebrating American Roots." The Smithsonian New Harmonies exhibit in Bremen featured different kinds of music. The Thomas A. Dorsey Choir was chosen to represent gospel music on the program organized by Dr. Keith Herbert from the University of West Georgia at Carrolton. We sang at the New England Conservatory of Music in Boston, Massachusetts, for two consecutive years, and we also sang at the original House of Blues each time we were in Boston. The people stayed after the brunch to hear us sing, and they said they really enjoyed us. We also sang in Chicago for their Black History celebration in February.

KK: Have you sung in the State of Georgia as well?

SM: Yes. We have been invited to sing at weddings—a gospel choir at a wedding! We have sung in downtown Atlanta and at Buckhead. We sing for programs here in Villa Rica and the surrounding areas as well.

KK: And these are Caucasians?

SM: Yes, and after that, we were invited to sing at another wedding. We don't charge anything to sing. We sing just as hard at each occasion, whether we are paid or not. We just enjoy ministering to people. Eric, our minister of music, says, "You don't know what people are going through when you stand up to sing. You don't know what they've been through." Our pastor always says to smile at the people when you're singing to them and put your heart into it. (Dr. James E. Potts, Pastor, D.M., (with First Lady Sabrenia B. Potts) has served as pastor for twenty-seven years. He is the Northern Regional Vice-President of the General Missionary Baptist Convention of Georgia, Districts 5, 7, and 9, and also a member of the Thomas Dorsey Birthplace Foundation in Villa Rica, Georgia.)

KK: I was very impressed that your youth choir also sings hymns and clearly pronounces the words.

SM: That's one of the things Mt. Prospect is known for. We're going to sing a hymn on Sunday morning—I don't care what. That's another thing Eric always tells us: to pronounce our words... if you're talking to me, and I don't understand you, it's not doing either of us any good. He also makes sure we sing songs that carry a message....

KK: You certainly carry the legacy of Dr. Dorsey well in Villa Rica. It was very important to him that songs were sung with feeling and carried a message.

SM: I'm not a person who loves contemporary music. I heard a preacher once say, "that's all it is—temporary." I remember that the late Bishop Moales [President of the National Convention of Gospel Choirs and Choruses from 1993 to 2010] once said that when you're going through something, you don't want all this be-bop music. You want some "Amazing Grace," and "Precious Lord," and "Father I Stretch My Hands to Thee"....That's what we need. That's what brought our parents through, and that's what's keeping us now—those songs and prayers of our forefathers...and now we're [The Dorsey Birthplace Choir] continuing to do the same. Many people can claim this or that about his legacy, but no one else can say he was born in their town.

Dr. Lena McLin, Niece of Thomas A. Dorsey

(Personal Interview, April, 2014)

During the span of three months, Dr. Lena McLin, Thomas A. Dorsey's niece, granted the author permission to interview her on three separate occasions. McLin resides in a stately apartment condo in the South Shore neighborhood of Chicago. The living room is white with pictures on all walls. The most dramatic picture is a tile mosaic of Dr. Martin L. King, Jr, a childhood friend. The halls are covered with awards, pictures, and plaques. She conducts voice classes in her home on Saturdays. Seated behind a white grand piano, she teaches and instructs both individually and collectively. Her students' final grade is a performance at the annual "Tea with a Twist" sponsored as a scholarship vehicle for members of the Holy Vessels Baptist Church, which she pastors.

"Tea with a Twist" 2014 was held Saturday, July 12, 2014 at the Crerar Memorial Presbyterian Church's Community Hall. This church, at 8100 S. Calumet Avenue, located in the Chatham neighborhood of Chicago, takes pride in providing community outreach. Crerar was originally organized in March 1897 as a mission located near 59th Street and Indiana Avenue. Pastor Rev. Michael Miller stated that the community center, built in 1939, was available for programs that were of benefit to the neighborhood. The event was filled to overflowing—so much so that those arriving late were unable to find seating within the center.

Dr. McLin has a musical legacy of her own. She taught music at Kenwood High School in the Hyde Park neighborhood of Chicago for many years, cultivating the secular singing talents of students who included popular singers Chaka Khan and R. Kelly. She also composed lyrics and music for her students and started the McLin Singers, who still perform to this day. Her students achieved many accomplishments—among them, CD recordings—under her tutelage.

When the author first interviewed her, McLin was conducting her weekly Saturday group voice lesson to nine ladies. She coached them with the following words:

> Singing is sustained talking on a breath. Place thumbs on waist, thumbs in the front. Stand with one foot slightly in front of the other one. Stand on ball and heel. Take a breath, say "oh," hold it, sustain it, and sing your name in your tone. Singing is talking on air that you sustain.

Each student then presented a solo and was critiqued as to technique, emotion, style, key, and personal fit, i.e., whether the music was suited to her voice and range. She emphasized that they "sing your style." She accompanied one student on a classical selection, which the student sang in Italian. She exhorts her to repeat the words, "I've been blessed, and believe it. Music reflects everything you do," she says. "You can't sing in every place... everything in life has a song."

McLin expounded on the genre of classical music. "It takes six to eight years of training and practicing every day to sing opera, an aria. Classical singers must project their voices. They must sing without a microphone over the instruments in the orchestra. Their voices must be human instruments." She clarified the differences in some modes of performance. "A musical show may have dancing, singing, and speaking," she explained.

McLin spoke prophetically about one of her students, whom she advised to get a manager: "She could be the next Mary J. Blige, Aretha Franklin," she said. Chaka Khan, R. Kelly, Tammy McCann, and more singers than she can remember were students of hers when she taught music during her career as a Chicago Public School teacher.

"To be a church gospel singer you have to train yourself and have the Holy Ghost. You can't sing something that you don't believe. You have to study, and you have to believe."

One of Dr. McLin's favorite songs of her uncle's is one he wrote in the 1940s. She played and sang a portion of "I'm Going to Live the Life I Sing about in My Song." Dr. McLin has no tolerance for performances that lack the spirit of God. "Gospel shows are where people are yelling, shouting, and slobbering," she says.

A guest came in briefly, a former student, who now performs professionally on stage. She sang for those of us present: parents, significant others, as well as the students. Dr. McLin then privately counseled a student after the class ended about making wise decisions. She stressed the importance of discovering the career choice that is best for her. "You must think about what you want to be."

The author's last visit with Dr. Mc Lin took place July 18, 2014, at which she received, as a personal courtesy, family photographs for this book. They included a picture of the Dorsey family in Atlanta, Georgia; Professor and Mrs. Dorsey; Etta Plant Dorsey; and other pictures of Professor Thomas A. Dorsey. She also identified for the author the family members in the group picture and elaborated on each of their musical talents. (Her mother, the youngest Dorsey sibling, was also musically talented, and began training McLin at a very young age to serve in the church by sharing her musical gifts.)

McLin, an accomplished pianist in her own right, has written several musical selections as well as textbooks for student use in elementary, high school, and college. She has also written librettos for operas, arias, and cantatas. She related to the author a moving experience upon learning of the death of Dr. Martin Luther King, Jr., with whom she grew up in Atlanta.

They were both from Levitical families and were children of pastors. McLin's father, Rev. E. J. Johnson, was the pastor of Greater Mt. Calvary Baptist Church in the Mechanicsville neighborhood of Atlanta. She recalls receiving a phone call at her school from Dr. King after his famous March on Washington in 1963…"The school went wild," she recalls. "Someone came running to my room and said, "Dr. Martin Luther King is on the phone for you." She went to answer the phone.

"Free at Last" is a cantata she wrote immediately upon hearing of his death. One of her sisters had been at the home of Coretta Scott King when she received the call from the Secret Service that her husband had been shot. Mc Lin shared how deeply it affected her. She couldn't sleep or eat. The Lord gave her the words and the music for "Free at Last" all at once. She immediately sat down and began composing that memorial to his life. The words, "Free At Last," which are engraved above his tomb in Atlanta, are also included in her dedication to him.

McLin, additionally, has composed music for other U.S. presidents. Her anthem, a single song to John F. Kennedy, was entitled "The Torch Has Passed" [she added] "to a new generation of Americans." That anthem was one of the compositions rendered in Germany at the historic celebration of the fall of the Berlin Wall in 1989. Most recently, she composed an anthem for President Barack Obama. She recited from memory the poem "This Land," which she wrote and set to music.

The family's musical legacy continues in her daughter Beverly, an accomplished secular composer, and her grandson, who recently graduated from Columbia College in Chicago and who is also gifted in composing.

LM: I started an opera company—the McLin Opera Company. We
        gave operas every year—twice a year—for black people for
        about eight years. My husband was a fine baritone opera sing-
        er. He died about two years ago. [My uncle] would stop and
        sell his music at the railroad stations for five cents. He had to
        write out his own music. He had gone to the music schools
        up here. You see, it all goes back to his mother. She was a
        very learned woman. Her first husband, worked for the rail-
        road. He would get a chance to come to Chicago and New
        York. She would come to Chicago and New York on vacation
        and study music. They had an old pull organ with pedals in
        the house. Etta would play that organ. They had church in her
        house. Some said he was a deacon. She later married a Dor-
        sey. He was a preacher. She played for his church. His
        [Dorsey's] father taught at Morehouse.

KK: I knew he [Thomas Dorsey] went to Morehouse and had stud-
        ied with a teacher there.

LM: Yes. Then he came here and went to the Chicago Musical
        College. That's where he learned to pen his music, to write
        it out….When he got to Atlanta, he started going to the 81
        Theater down there and he starting jazzing it up, "bluesing"
        it up…and he became a great player. Dorsey could play like
        mad….He used to play for the house parties. They had a
        pianist come in. You paid for everything you ate. They had a
        little liquor, too. He became a big house party player. We
        lived at 6520 Vernon Avenue—right here in Chicago. I was

a little girl. He got a break. Ma Rainey was the "Queen of the Blues." She hired Dorsey. He formed a band and wrote all her music.

He met a beautiful girl [Nettie] there and married her. He started writing these gospel songs. He was really carried away with them.... [After the death of his wife Nettie and baby son], he called my mother and said, "Send Lena Mae up here 'cause I have to have a child around here...." I'm the oldest, so they sent me up here, and I stayed with my uncle until I got in junior high school. He gave me piano lessons. He hired the people from the conservatory to come to the house and train me from a little child. I got to be a classical musician and was known as a child prodigy. I could play anything. I have a sister who is an opera singer.

KK: Now, did you attend Pilgrim?

LM: Yes. J.C. Smith, Sr., baptized me at age seven. I knew everybody. I sang. I used to hang out with Sallie Martin, Roberta Martin, and Mahalia Jackson. I didn't like to go with Mahalia because she used to dip snuff. She would have snuff, and I would be embarrassed. I didn't want the kids at McCosh or anyone else to know I knew someone like that....

KK: Your grandmother lived with you?

LM: She did all the cooking and raised me with the fear of the Lord and also Lovie, his sister, lived with us.

KK: What are some of your fondest memories of your uncle?

LM: My fondest memory is of his character. He was always so
        kind—never raised his voice... even when he was training
        Sallie Martin and Mahalia...he just talked to them. He was a
        quiet man. He didn't like confusion. If the church had con-
        fusion, he'd leave. He loved peace. If he saw you on the street,
        and you didn't have a ride, he'd give you a ride and most
        likely give you some money...even when he came to give us
        a whipping....My sister Thelma lived with us for a while....
        He'd have the strap in his hand. We'd go under the bed, and
        when he left, we made a beeline down the stairs and into the
        backyard.

KK: How did he dress?

LM: He was an immaculate dresser. You never saw him without a
        shirt and a tie. The shirt was always white.

KK: Do you believe that Levitical families who lead in worship
        are generational? Do they still exist today?

LM: Yes. My father was a minister. My brother was a minister.
        You see it. You can't miss it. Music is in all in them.

KK: What is something you would want to share with gospel
        singers today in terms of their legacy, their history, their
        purpose?

LM: I think their purpose is very necessary. They are very

necessary. I just wish they would stop trying to scream.
It's not necessary. We sang, but we didn't tear up our
vocal chords…The feeling that you got to overdo….

KK: Does that have something to do with the accompaniment
being too loud?

LM: That's actually it. It has to do with the instruments you use…
you can't hear the singers. Now people…it seems like
the gospel singers now are pitching their songs too high.
They are reaching above their capability of feeling and
producing. They are loud….

KK: I read an article recently by a young man who wrote that we
should recognize that gospel music is dead and just hold the
funeral. He said gospel artists are now signing on to secular
record labels.

LM: That's what they're doing. They're imitating the world's style
and calling everything "gospel." They are singing like the
world's style. They are not singing gospel. Gospel music…
anything they can take to make it black—to make it a new
day a new way in blackness—and, as a result, they are mur-
dering everything that historically has made them. Do you
understand what I mean now? They are killing gospel music.
They don't worship God anymore….They worship development and organization. Gospel music is what my uncle created—Thomas A. Dorsey. He created a preaching style in
singing like the preacher was singing….The preacher start-

ed singing (she demonstrates the style)....He took that part of it and made what?

KK: Songs?

LM: Music. Now, he was limited because he didn't know anything but the blues. He was limited to the blues. I can give you an example of what he did that [is] going on now. He took to telling the gospel singers that they got to live the life they sing about in their songs. But he plays it in the blues...and all the shows....He would go in there and sell drinks and pop-corn in order to be around the blues players and musicians... and that's how he learned to sing. Here's one of his favorite songs.

(Dr. McLin then goes to the piano and plays and sings "I'm Going to Live the Life I Sing About in My Song.")

Dr. Lena McLin
(Personal Interview, May, 2014)

KK: What is your experience with Pilgrim Baptist Church?

LM: As a girl I got baptized there at seven by Dr. Junius Smith, Sr. I went to rehearsal with my uncle....

KK: What were his rehearsals like?

LM: They were interesting. He kept people in the right voice, with the right training; with the right interpretations...He didn't like put-ons. He'd have a fit if you were putting on airs. He felt if you really felt the music, felt the text, and you really knew what you were talking about, that you would feel the spirit, and the spirit would come in. It was interesting.

KK: Did Sallie Martin ever play for his choir?

LM: No. She'd come sometimes to rehearsals, but you know, she had her own group—The Sallie Martin Singers. They were good. I thought they were good.

KK: She did a lot to help the National Convention of Gospel Choirs and Choruses as she went around the country organizing and recruiting.

LM: I think she did a lot, but it was mainly Uncle Ted [Dorsey] sitting around the house telling her what to do.

KK: Although he didn't go, he taught her?

LM: Well, he couldn't go. He was going other places. Actually, he ran a business. He ran a studio. They bought music from him, and they would send him money through the mail. He had a secretary, his brother Lloyd, and some other people. They would package the music and send it in the mail. People would pay for it. So he really had the first music studio for a black man that I think I had ever seen. He made a fortune.... Sallie would stay on the tour, and he would stay home and take care of the business....I remember Magnolia Butts from Metropolitan. She was very good. She would help keep things going....Mr. Frye... all of them would help to keep the thing going.

(Dr. McLin then shared the highlight of the convention [to her]—his address to NCGCC.)

LM: Dorsey would give his annual address at the convention. He would preach. He was a minister....He would stay on the singers to live the life they sing about in their song. He would illustrate those things. He would make the singers illustrate what they were talking about. They had to feel the spirit.

KK: I didn't think he became a minister until later on in life.

LM: No, he was really a minister to start with. [But] he didn't want to own it. You could see it in his early life....The music just brought it out of him...although he was writing blues, playing in the house parties, but he was a man who never violated God's laws. He was a quiet man, but he was very observant. He observed everything.

KK: How did he choose the people who sang for him? I know how Sallie Martin became his spokeswoman. How did Mahalia Jackson fit in the picture?

LM: She used to live next door to his studio. She was a hairdresser. She'd come over and get some refreshments, and she just started singing, and he just started teaching her.

KK: Who are other disciples that he taught to sing the Dorsey way?

LM: There were so many....Willie Mae Ford Smith—she could sing a whole concert of gospel songs and set the church on fire—and she would go all over the country....There was another man. He was blind, I think. I can't think of his name.... He'd tear up the convention, and Dorsey would say, "Praise God—that's the stuff, that's the stuff." I can hear him saying that now....He formed the Dorsey Singers: Marion Peebles, Ms. Alexander...I can't remember, but I can see them in my mind's eye....He was more about going around and starting gospel choirs and teaching people how the gospel music went.

KK: Like an apostle of music.

LM: Yes. He went around just like Jesus' men. He would go, and he would really teach...he didn't want no yelling. It was beautiful. You were certainly touched.

KK: There are reports that he had a nervous breakdown about the time your mother let you come to live with him.

LM: He didn't have a nervous breakdown. I heard those reports, but they are not true. People who don't know the Lord don't know how the Holy Ghost deals with you. God was dealing with him. He never had a nervous breakdown, but people don't understand the Holy Ghost dealing with him. He gave his all to the blues and to the gospel...he was torn between two worlds....We would have known. We were right there in that house. He would pray and thank God for what He had provided for us.

(Dr. McLin then talked about the rules growing up in his house. The meals were prepared. There was a certain time to eat. They had to be clean. She related a story about sneaking to eat strawberries with her sister Thelma and getting caught by "Uncle Ted." They had put their sandy hands into the strawberries.)

LM: We were scared. We were so dumb. We didn't think they would know that we had put our hands into the strawberries. He always had the lady to come in and help Aunt Kathryn.

KK: Was that after his mother left?

LM: His mother stayed with them all the time. She only went back to Atlanta when she thought she was going to die. She then went back to Atlanta to die near where her husband had been. She died in my house. Her mother's grandmother had to sneak her children—eight or nine of them (half of them were white) out of Villa Rica. She put them on a haystack wagon and put hay all over them and got them past the guard…. That's how they moved to Atlanta. The ones that she brought back [now] live in California. After she died, they disowned us because they were white, and we never did see them any-more…. I don't know what her mama's name was—she was Etta Dorsey's mother …but I know she had the half-and-half children. We don't know how many children she had…. My sister had information on them, but she died. I know one day a woman came up to me and said that she was my cous-in, and she was white.…My grandmother had a sister that was black like us. She lived in Villa Rica, too. My grandmoth-er was a smart woman. She was first married to another man. He worked for the railroad. He made good money. He would send her up here [Chicago] and to New York. She studied music there. Her next husband was a preacher. She had an organ that you pumped. She would play it for the services. That's what she trained Uncle Ted on.

Rev. Dr. Gregory P. Nelson

(Personal Interview, August, 2014)

Dr. Gregory P. Nelson is the pastor of the Delaine-Waring AME Church at 680 Swan Street, Buffalo, New York. He has a Doctor of Divinity degree from Aidan University in Jacksonville, Florida. He is the national assistant chaplain to NCGCC, a teacher in the Artelia Hutchins Institute, and a member of the Pastoral Alliance Department. Dr. Nelson has sung with groups around the New Jersey area, where he grew up. He also has sung with the Philadelphia and New Jersey Mass Choirs. In addition, he has written music for choir recordings in the late 1980s. He is a pastor with an appreciation and passion for music—especially sacred music in the black church. In this interview, Nelson gives his definition of sacred music in the black church.

GN: There is some wonderful music that we share in the black church that sounds nice but isn't necessarily sacred. If it doesn't point me to Christ, his death, burial, and resurrection, [it isn't sacred]....When I think about sacred music, I think about music that draws my mind to Christ...it's taking me somewhere...to a place that points to God. Inspirational music can take you anywhere it's designed to take you, but sacred music takes you to a certain place, to a certain person.

[The] Latin [term] "Sanctus" [bears the] concept of sacrament, so sacred music in the black church is very clear and very defined... [it is] music that we share in our churches that points to Sanctus, the sacred. When it points to God, Christ, Lord, the Savior, the blood, the empty tomb, the Trinity, to the blood-drenched ground of Calvary-that helps us understand sacred music.

> We have to become more serious about lifting up the standards of sacred music in the Black Church and holding on to the tenets that makes music sacred. We need to begin to teach young people about sacred music in the Black Church.... We have about three or four decades of persons that haven't visited sacred music. We've moved away from anthems, from spirituals. Young people don't know anything about meter hymns....They had a profound message and purpose in the Black Church.

> Thomas Dorsey was able to make that cross from blues [and] from secular, but he rested at the sacred music, the gospel music....I believe all along that he was making his journey— even in the other music that may have been considered secular. If you listen to his other music intently, there was always a hint of gospel in his music, even before we labeled it as that. I think this convention [the NCCGC] has done a wonderful job trying to revisit sacred music in the Black Church and preserve it in the Black Church. We've given it definition; now we need to be true to it and bring it back.

(Dr. Nelson discusses the course he teaches during the convention on sacred music. There is now in place a three-year certification process between NCGCC and the Washington, D.C. Theological Seminary for continuing education credit. He will teach this in his course on Sacred Music in the Black Church. He will lift up, not redefine sacred music in the black church.)

103

KK: If I understand your definition, then sacred music is all music that points to God, to Christ, to salvation, and it includes

gospel, along with our spirituals, our hymns, and our anthems. Our job for the twenty-first century is to educate our youth. We must convey to them the full understanding of the African American religious experience that Thomas Dorsey tried to bring into the church so that our music would reflect the life of the people, and the things they were going through at that time, especially in Chicago.

GN: What we have to understand about music is that anything that stops evolving dies. Although it continues to evolve, there are still some basic tenets, some basic structures that never change. Sacred music takes me somewhere. Inspirational music can be somewhat ambiguous....Sacred music constantly leads me to Christ—always. We are happy to serve that congregation [Delaine-Waring AME Church] at this time in history, and we are excited about helping that congregation understand the importance of revisiting—not redefining—sacred music in the Black Church. I want to make sure we get it right when it comes to music in the Black Church—especially sacred music—that we understand and embrace—not redefine—[but] re-visit [sacred music]. My prayer for the new generation of musicians, songwriters, pastors, and singers is that they understand that sacred music sits in a class all by itself and that there are certain tenets that help us understand that this can only be sacred music and nothing else, although it continues to evolve.

Dr. Bessie M. Palmer

(Personal Interview, August 2014)

Dr. Bessie M. Palmer is the Second Vice-President of the National Convention of Gospel Choirs and Choruses. She has a love and passion for this convention and the people of God she has interacted with over the last 57 years. She is the third national organizer within the 81-year history of the convention and president of the Louisville Choral Union.

KK: How did you become a part of this convention?

BP: My president from Louisville, Kentucky, would always talk about the Convention of Gospel Choirs and Choruses; in fact, it was the highlight of her year. Mr. Floyd Adams was the organist/pianist, and Mr. Ronald Ford, the director, would always talk about going to the National Convention of Gospel Choirs and Choruses. Then there was a senior director, Barbara Brown Elliott, who would always talk about it. Finally, in 1957, I joined the Louisville Gospel Choral Union. That year we hosted the National Convention of Gospel Choirs and Choruses in Louisville, Kentucky. We were not into hotels at that time, so the entire convention met at the Broadway Temple AMEZ Church located at Thirteenth and Broadway Streets. The parent body met in the sanctuary, and the youth department met in their dining area in the back. We had a glorious time. From that time on I was hooked. God has blessed me to attend every convention but one since 1957....I treasure every moment of this convention. It has proven to be everything that they told me it was. I thank God for the life lessons I have learned, and I thank God for the experience.

KK: You have held several offices in the National Convention of Gospel Choirs and Choruses. You are now the Second Vice-President and the National Organizer.

BP: Yes. I started there as an assistant recording secretary in the Youth and Young Adults Department. Dr. Mary Wilks was the president. Then, I moved to the Alumni Chorale—the group organized to keep us on board (the group that was too old to stay in the Youth and Young Adult Department). That proved to be a lifeline for me because that just piqued my interest. Mrs. Sallie Martin supported Dr. Earl Preston, Jr., who used to be the chairman of the board of this convention. He helped to promote the Alumni Chorale when it first got started. At that time, Mother Beatrice Brown was still supervisor, and she asked that the youth department would stay intact until the age of thirty, so I was well past [that] age before I graduated from the Youth Department. I held the office of financial secretary for the National Alumni Chorale.

There are age restrictions for everything. At that time it was forty-five (the Alumni Chorale). The convention was held again in Louisville. In 1986, the convention was at the Gault House. By that time, we had moved into hotels. They had a graduation that year. I graduated from the Alumni Chorale into just the parent body and began to run for office. The first office I held was fourth vice-president, and then I must have run for the next office—the third—and finally the second vice-presidency became available, and I was glad to run for it.

I have been a vice-president ever since the early 1980s in one of those positions. Bishop Moales, when he was elected president, invited presidents into the boardroom. We learned more about what was going on. That was a joy. I appreciated that. He was the one who appointed me as national organizer. I served after Sallie Martin and Dorothy Grant. I have enjoyed that position. I'm excited about telling people about this convention because I believe in it wholeheartedly. This is one of the best conventions. This is the mother convention. I enjoy telling everyone about the convention. I can even remember the times when James Cleveland would come by and do things with this convention. He talked about his connection to this convention and about Dr. Dorsey and Mrs. Sallie Martin. It's been a blessing. I challenge anyone who loves gospel music and the Lord to come and be connected. This was a semi-honeymoon in Chicago for me and my husband in 1965. That's how much I think about this convention.

KK: Did you know Dr. Dorsey personally?

BP: Dr. Dorsey would come to Louisville for anniversaries at the Zion Baptist Church, where Dr. M. L. King, Jr.'s brother pastored for a little while. We would have our anniversary on the third Sunday in March. He [Dr. Dorsey] would go to our director's home. She would bring out the real china and the real silver, and we would go have dinner with Dr. Dorsey.

That was my personal connection with him. We would sit down and dine with him.

BP: I remember once when my musician was playing his song. Dr. Dorsey was working with us. He said, "No, it goes like this. I ought to know. I wrote it." He would stay at the president's home—Zenobia Harris's. Sallie Martin came after he was no longer able to travel. She came to my home church programs in Jeffersonville, Indiana. I'm proud that she was over there at First Trinity. I praise God for that.

KK: What do you think Dr. Dorsey would think about the transition in the music of today from his time? Do you think he would be pleased?

BP: I think he would be pleased. He was a great blues man. They did not like the music that he had. I think that he would be very receptive. I think he would want us to keep it real—to make sure that it glorified God...I think we need to learn that all music isn't for all occasions. My favorite is still traditional gospel, but I can appreciate all of it. I can understand the rap because my son...learned the books of the Bible from a young man who did a gospel rap....I think Dr. Dorsey would embrace all of it, but he always taught us to do whatever we were doing in a dignified manner—so that it glorifies God. (Palmer shares the vision of Dr. Moales in appointing President Gentry as his first vice-president for the convention.)

BP: I remember Marabeth Gentry being in the Youth and Young Adult Department. When she —her father was first vice-president when I first became president— came back, (she was touring in Europe) she got even closer with what was going on. Bishop Moales appointed her as his first vice-president. I have to believe that God had given him the revelation to move her to this position. He told us in a board meeting one time that he didn't plan to hold that office for life....We see now that God had anointed this man and put into his sight what needed to be done. He told us once that "anyone who doesn't prepare for someone to [follow] him prepares to fail." I feel like he prepared her to succeed him....

KK: How many choral unions belong to the National Convention of Gospel Choirs and Choruses?

BP: There are somewhere in the neighborhood of forty-five to fifty unions. We invite new unions to come [join] in April during our board meeting or in August for the most part, to set them up for installations. Most of them already have their choirs formed. Some of them start from scratch. I give them directions on how to start a union. Every union must have structure. There must be a parent body of members ages 26 and up.

KK: I know there are some five-generational families here. The Cummings family is one. Do you know of others?

BP: I know Bishop Moales was brought by his grandmother, so that makes four generations. My family would make four generations. There are many four-generation families here. I think

Mr. Cummings is somewhat unique, with five generations (Generations of NCGCC families were recognized during the NCGCC 80th Annual Session and included in the session's program).

KK: What is your favorite Dorsey hymn?

BP: "Precious Lord." I think that's about everyone's.

Mrs. Joy Pearson
(Phone Interview, January, 2014)

Joy Pearson is one of the oldest living members of Pilgrim Baptist Church in Chicago. She was a member of Pilgrim even before Thomas Dorsey became a member. She migrated to Chicago with her family from Mississippi in December 1925 when she was nine years old and has been there ever since. She celebrated her ninety-ninth birthday in 2014. She still travels to family functions and recalls visits to her mother's family in Mississippi during summer vacations.

Pearson grew up on the south side of Chicago, where she attended Willard Elementary School and Hyde Park High School. She graduated from Peters Business College, where she took elementary bookkeeping and Gregg shorthand. She worked at Cook County Hospital for thirty-five years as a secretary in the OB/GYNY department.

KK: What do you remember about Thomas Dorsey as a member of Pilgrim when he first came to your church?

JP: He wrote popular songs. Rev. Austin invited him to join. Pastor Junius Austin, Sr., gave him permission to organize the first gospel chorus. Mabel Mitchell was the church secretary and pianist. There were three yearly concerts—spring, pre-Thanksgiving, and one before the National Convention. The gospel choir rehearsed on the same night as the other choirs.

KK: Where did the choir sing?

JP: They sang in the balcony because the choir stand couldn't hold them. A choir stand was built for them [later]. They had cornets and drums as well. His wife found him at Pilgrim.

KK: Is there anything else that comes to mind about Professor Dorsey?

JP: The way he could direct, play, and his voice.

Rev. Morris and Dr. Eva Purnell
(Personal Interview, July, 2014)

Dr. Eva J. Purnell, an early gospel legend, was honored at the 2007 Chicago Gospel Fest as a "living gospel legend." She is minister-of-music emeritus at Memorial M.B. Church in Chicago. She was a member of the pioneering Inspirational Singers with Almond Dawson. The group was one of the early pioneer gospel groups presented and hosted by Sid Ordower on his show "Jubilee Showcase." It was the first program dedicated to gospel music in the country. Her husband, Rev. Morris Purnell, was a member of Pilgrim Baptist Church as a boy. Pilgrim was the family church. His sister, Marion Purnell Peebles, was a member of the Dorsey Trio called The Celestial Sing-

111

ers. They share recollections of gospel music in Chicago and of Professor Thomas Dorsey.

EP: Morris knew Thomas Dorsey from his sister. He was over to her house all the time. Marion was a great hostess, and she entertained. (Musicians, singers and directors met frequently over dinner during those days. Their friendship extended beyond the church walls. There was a sense of community and kinship among gospel singers).

EP: People from the South didn't want to hear that kind of music [Dorsey's]. They were trying to get away from that and felt they were too sophisticated for that in their worship service. Dorsey was too "bluesy." His chords were too bluesy. Big churches didn't like it.

MP, EP: He was a great director. He really wasn't a singer, but he was a very disciplined director. Dorsey's music wasn't to be changed. You were to play it like it was written. Soloists didn't adlib. Musicians didn't improvise.

KK: I found out that gospel music really did begin at Ebenezer with Theodore Frye as director and Thomas Dorsey as pianist.

EP: Theodore Frye was known for directing. He was no singer.

MP, EP: They [churches, organizations, and individuals] had great respect for Thomas Dorsey. They called him "Mr. Dorsey." The National Baptist Convention respected him because he was published. I don't think Frye had published then. He [Dorsey] didn't want to sing on the downbeat. He was so precise. There was no such thing as someone doing this and someone else doing that. You had to attend rehearsal. If he called a soloist, and you didn't learn it [the selected song], he would sit you down and get someone else because you didn't want to sing. Churches believed in singing hymns. Sallie [Martin] was a blues style singer. I know he trained her. She had that style. Roberta [Martin] was smoother, classier. Everyone had to know a Dorsey song. [His singers] called him "Mr. Dorsey," out of respect—never "Thomas." They respected soloists— even if they didn't like them. Those people didn't just make choirs—they made soloists. You could brag, "I sang before Dorsey." Today, people don't even know his name.

Today we let people do whatever they want to do. Everyone [then] had to sing the same note. If one went down, all went down. Dorsey could do a concert of just his own material and hymns. No one was going to do a concert without hymns. Now you go to church, and they don't know hymns. Musicians can't play hymns. Memorial has stayed with hymns, but now Baptist churches don't do hymns.

EP: I went to a workshop in the 1960s or 1970s. I sang for The Gospel Music Workshop of America [Mass Choir]. I was a movie star. I sang James Cleveland's style. I didn't sing my style. Then it was the director and the choir. People now aren't willing to be a part of the choir. They want to be a star. They sang in the balcony. They didn't get any money. You think back to Motown. It wasn't the person, it was the group.

MP: [Of his early years at Pilgrim Baptist Church, Morris Purnell says] I would have to attend church so that I could go to the show. I'd make sure my sister [Marion Peebles] saw me. I'd go up to the balcony and wait for her to see me. I'd wave. I'd let her see me somewhere in the back. Then I was out the door.

(Eva shared the sense of community felt by gospel singers. The Thompson Community Singers and the Southside Community Choir were the two best known gospel choirs in Chicago. They frequently appeared together on concerts.)

EP: You'd be so proud to be part of an organization. You'd say with great pride, "I'm a Tommie." They were known for their presentation and precision. They had order. They would stand in line for minutes without talking. We stand before an audience now…no way. We rehearsed for hours. We had to make sure we had it perfected.

EP: [Eva remembered a concert of the Thompson Community Singers]. They'd sing a song that they sang five years ago. When they called that song, "'Tis the Old Ship of Zion," everybody sang it—like they had done it yesterday. Clay Wilborn was famous for directing "Down by the Riverside." He wasn't invited up to sing; he was invited up to direct. [Rev.] Clay Evans's sister, [Dr. Lou Della Reid], was known for directing. She directed "It Is Well." They will honor her as the director. She could direct the whole church. We've lost that.

KK: I thought the big choir sound started with James Cleveland. You're saying it started with Thomas Dorsey.

114

EP: The choir sound started with Dorsey. Dorsey was strictly blue-sy. Cleveland took it up a notch. His chord changes were at a higher level. They were a progressive style. Hawkins took it to another level—a contemporary style. Hawkins integrated the sacred with the secular sound.

KK: What do you think about mixing secular and sacred?

EP: That's a bad thing, because if they didn't say "Jesus," you wouldn't know it wasn't a secular song. Some churches sing secular songs.

KK: People get caught up in the beat. They don't know the message or the messenger. Thanks for sharing.

Ms. Yvonne Salter
(Personal Interview, May, 2014)

Yvonne Salter, church financial secretary, grew up in Ebenezer Missionary Baptist Church at a time when it was one of the most influential black churches in Chicago. She has been a member of Ebenezer since infancy and can remember many things that took place over the years, including wooden seats, filled to capacity—even rooms on the sides that sometimes were used as overflow rooms when the balcony and downstairs were filled. Says Salter:

> Junior Church was held for the kids. Membership declined after the large apartment buildings were slowly torn down in the mid-sixties. The relationship between the Vacation Bible School, which served the neighborhood children and the church family, was

115

very close. The majority of Ebenezer's members are now in their eighties and nineties.

(Salter is still very active with a club that meets weekly who served as her mentors. She asserts that the church has endured so much and struggles to bring the community back to church. The task in the twenty-first century is bringing in the young to carry on. Now with landmark status, the church must go on, she says. Ebenezer Church went through an extensive process to obtain that landmark status. Salter recalls):

> ...and when we found out that our name...really was not officially on there [the landmark list], that's when we decided to pursue...that's when we filled out the application, got with the board....They came down here and gave us a list of everything we had to do to prove that we were a landmark....So that's when we tried to find all the information we could possibly find at the church. We even went downtown to research when we purchased the church—the whole thing. We had to work with so much material....We got a lot of stuff together...I could probably pull out material and share it with you.

(Salter commented on the controversy surrounding the church that carries the title of "The Birthplace of Gospel Music.")

> This was a question addressed by the committee as they pursued landmark status. One of the first church-es to embrace gospel music, "Ebenezer is the birth-place of gospel music," says Salter, lifelong member, financial secretary, and member of the landmark

committee, "and Pilgrim Baptist Church is the home of gospel music."

Professor Frye was our director, and Thomas Dorsey was his assistant and also the pianist. I know they were the ones who were working together to develop our first Adult Gospel Choir and Young Adult Choir, and I know eventually, after a while, Dorsey had left here and went to Pilgrim. (The Ebenezer Senior Gospel Chorus was organized on December 6, 1931, by the late Dr. James Howard Lorenzo Smith, according to Ebenezer Archives).

Dr. Nathan L. Schaffer, Jr.

(Personal Interview, September, 2014)

Dr. Nathan L. Schaffer, Jr., is a Levitical leader who currently serves as a shepherd and pastor of the Memorial Missionary Baptist Church in Chicago, Illinois. He has served as a worship leader, musician, singer, and arranger and chorale organizer. His appreciation for hymns and anthems began at a traditional "silk-stocking" church—Berean Baptist Church in Chicago, where his grandmother was the pianist for the gospel choir. It was where he also first heard Dr. Dorsey and Roberta Martin songs.

He became the organist for the gospel choir at the age of sixteen, playing on a spinet organ purchased with S & H green stamps. Nathan also directed the choir at Vernon Baptist Church before becoming the organist and minister of music at the Antioch Baptist Church in Chicago. After graduating from Englewood High School, he organized the

117

Nathan L. Schaffer Chorale, which began as a group of five members from Vernon Baptist Church and grew to more than twenty singers. He has conducted music workshops throughout the nation, and he is a teacher in the Progressive Baptist Convention. Dr. Schaffer became the pastor of the Memorial M.B. Church in 1996. He also serves as Dean of Students at the Chicago Baptist Institute International.

KK: What is your definition of sacred music?

NS: Sacred music is any music that pertains to God—basically, the lyrics. It gives you a sense of God.

KK: What is your opinion of sacred music in the twenty-first century?

NS: Sacred music in the twenty-first century has really expanded and evolved. Some of that isn't good [because] it has done away with more foundational sacred music [anthems, spirituals, hymns] in place of more contemporary music.
        Many churches—historical and stalwart churches in the Atlanta, Georgia area, for example—no longer have [foundational music]… [A gifted musician] and member of the church who is also on the staff of a prestigious college, is no longer the music director because the new pastor wanted a more contemporary type of music....Another historical church in Baltimore, Maryland, had a tremendous long-standing history [of traditional sacred music], [which] they no longer have.... The new pastor wanted a more contemporary sound…There's room at the table for all of it.

KK: Do we need to address the concern that many twenty-first century musicians don't know anthems and hymns and do not read music?

NS: That certainly needs to be addressed. Our need to satisfy [church membership]—to have someone on the instrument— has caused this [problem]. (Schaffer speaks of churches held hostage by the worship leader/musician.)

NS: They will play here, but they have to leave at a certain time to go to the next church. No commitment. They get their check from the deacon as they walk out of the door. Many of the white congregations have gone to technology... the choirs sing from tracks. We, in the African American community, have not embraced that—we're afraid of that.

        This has really hampered development—spiritual development in the church. They [twenty-first century musicians] see no need to read music or learn an anthem—but, of course, if you can't read it, you can't play it....

KK: What do you think of "praise and worship" teams—not as a good or bad thing, but because they replace the meter hymns deacons sung in the devotional service? Children of the twenty-first century don't know hymns.

NS: Music should not be either or; it should be inclusive. Now we are totally in an era where many of our children don't know long and short meter hymns. That is something I have addressed in our church. Pastors need to be able to do that. Our children are growing up who have no knowledge of hymns.

(Schaffer refers to the mentoring that is present among Levitical pastor/priests and Levitical worship leaders/musicians through conferences and seminars.)

NS: That is so necessary and I'm glad to see it broadening in places like Chicago...remote areas don't always have it. Those seminars are so important.

KK: Did you know Dr. Dorsey personally?

NS: No, not by a personal handshake, but I have been in his presence two or three times, once or twice when I was young. I was at Pilgrim Baptist Church [the last time] when he was directing....his mind was slipping then, but he was still there. I saw him shortly before he passed away. Just to see him doing that meant so much to me. I've had the privilege of living to physically see Dr. Dorsey, physically see Mahalia Jackson, physically see Roberta Martin, and physically see James Cleveland—the whole gamut...that means so much to me.

KK: Chicago has such a rich gospel heritage. I know you know Inez Andrews. Albertina Walker has come here [to Memorial] because of you. You've told me we need to address issues in our churches; we need to have more seminars to mentor our musicians.... If there is one thing you could do right now to instantly change the impact of gospel music to the world, what would it be?

NS: To make sure that these very talented young musicians of today learn some form of music and write it down, put it on

paper....I've been to Sallie Martin's house and heard her story
of how she would sing the Dorsey songs and would stand
outside the church and sell the music—that's why it's still here
with us today. If they [today's twenty-first century musicians]
would incorporate some of that...Hawkins and Andrae
Crouch did that....if they would write it down—that would be
so wonderful.

KK: What can we do to increase the impact of gospel music for
salvation? You now don't know if the music you hear is secular or sacred unless you hear the word "Jesus." I wonder if
that impacts the twenty-first century generation—not having a
true foundation [of the African American religious experi-
ence].

NS: Oh, certainly it does. They need to go back to scripturally
based songs....The "Man Upstairs" could be Mr. Jones on the
eighth floor, the fifteenth floor... but I know why they don't do
it. I understand why these groups don't do it.

KK: Could you tell me why?

NS: They want to appeal to a crossover [audience]. The record
companies that pretty much own them say, "Okay, you can do
your Holy Ghost hallelujahs, but we have to sell some records." They [gospel artists] become hostages. That's my interpretation of that.

KK: So you are saying that the gospel artists, as well as the churches, have become hostages?

121

NS: Yes, they certainly have, and that's a shame.   It's because of money, and one might say this is jaded, but they [gospel artists] might want to live like Madonna, and that's fine because we should live as well as God has blessed us...but we must always remember that we have a message, and we must always perpetuate that message in the songs that we sing. I don't want to have to guess about what you're singing. It has nothing to do with the tempo—it doesn't matter the beat.... Sacred music is lyrics that pertain to God.

KK: That means that rap and hip hop is fine as long as it pertains to God.

NS: Let's call His name. Make it scriptural. We have to be able to identify ourselves. They didn't like Dr. Dorsey's music at first. I came out of a church that turned up their noses at him—a "silk-stocking" church that said, "Oh no, we don't like this music...." But now everybody sings it because he was persistent.... But more, it was a calling from God.

(Schaffer speaks of the necessity of seeing God through multidimensional lenses. There is the reality of God consciousness at the community level [the communal struggles of African Americans] as well as the personal intuitive level of consciousness as a personal 'I' experience with the God of the Twenty-third Psalm.)

NS: I take it even further than that. We sing of God in the third person. Sing "I am a friend of God." These are the things that connect us personally with God.

Professor Arnold Sevier, Pilgrim Baptist Church Musician

(Personal Interview, May, 2014)

Arnold Sevier is the music director for the historic Pilgrim Baptist Church in Chicago, the home church of the "Father of Gospel Music," Thomas A. Dorsey. Professor Sevier wasn't a member of Pilgrim during the life of Thomas A. Dorsey. He, nevertheless, coordinates, writes and arranges music for the church's Sanctuary Choir. Sevier, a gifted musician who plays all keyboards, and is a composer and arranger, shared his thoughts about gospel music.

AS: My first musical influence was Jean Henry Yokeley. She directed the junior and youth choirs at Greater Bethesda Church. Three men served as role models in the late 1950s and early 1960s: Herman Taylor, Irving Bunton, and Robert Morris. They taught me what I know about music. I was also influenced by Florence Madison-Stith. She became the minister of music after Irving Bunton. Robert Morris was one of the best choral conductors I know—white or black.

I grew up in the Morgan Park neighborhood of Chicago. I graduated from Shoop Elementary School and Morgan Park High School. I traveled extensively around the world while attending Kennedy-King Jr. College. The play, "Salt and Pepper," took us to Japan, Korea, and the Philippines. We [college students] toured parts of Asia for eight weeks.

KK: What did you do after graduation from Kennedy-King College?

AS:

I went to Jackson State University in Jackson, Mississippi. I

123

received a bachelor's degree in piano performance and a bachelor's degree in music education.

KK: How did you make your way to Pilgrim?

AS: I have a very dear friend, Al Carrington, who, when I left my last church, Mission of Faith, told me that they [Pilgrim] were looking for a musician....That was about ten years ago.

KK: Did you know Professor Dorsey?

AS: No. I never got to meet him personally. My father used to go to his house on Sunday...That was a phenomenon then. A lot of church people went to each other's houses discussing the Word and their own personal writings. That was a very special developmental time for gospel music. My father, Carl Edward Sevier, was his [Dr. Dorsey's] friend. My father was a singer and director. He was the hymn leader of Hope Bible Church on 58th and Lafayette Streets...but those old men knew the Word.

KK: What did you still find of the Dorsey legacy when you got here [Pilgrim]?

AS: We were still across the street then. They had music from 1915. I can't describe the feeling I had when I found out there was a fire....There were the old vintage pianos...all that music.... His family has what's left now. They are very lovely people. They are helping us to develop Professor Dorsey's legacy at-large. He did write some blues as well. He was a very well-rounded man.

That's why I really am proud to be here now—in such illustrious shoes. I have a banner to hold up, which is a challenge. One of my favorite scriptures is Philippians 4:13: "I can do all things through Christ who strengthens me." When I came here, I really wanted to develop the Dorsey tribute (the annual program honoring Dr. Dorsey's legacy) more. It still amazes me. My God, what a wonder Thou art!

KK: What is your favorite Dorsey song?

AS: "Precious Lord." My own arrangement of [the song] is now published and copy written with Abingdon Press. It's available for anyone who wants to purchase it. My arrangement has gone around the planet. I'm not a prolific writer. That arrangement was sung at Harold Washington's funeral as well as at Walter Cronkite's funeral.

(It was also performed at the 2014 commencement ceremony of the Gospel Music Workshop of America's Thurston Frazier Chorale (47th annual convention held in Atlanta, GA). Sevier proudly recalls its composition).

AS: There's a story about how I wrote it. When I went to sleep that night, I had a dream about a choir singing a really lush eight-part harmony, a double choir. It woke me up. Every time I closed my eyes, it would get louder. I got up and wrote a few notes so I wouldn't forget it. That was in 1969, and, as they say, the rest is history.

KK: What would you wish was different in music today?

AS: Music today has gone to another level. I wish that [there] wasn't so much hype. The emphasis [should be] placed on reaching the lost. What are we doing as Christians to exemplify God's Word, His principles, and His plan for this world? I met Donnie McClurkin and Richard Smallwood in college. But the purpose of our music comes originally from Professor Dorsey. Its [purpose] was to reach the common man, [so that] some of everybody could say I know a man who can save everybody.

KK: Do you feel the artists today really believe what they sing, or is it about money?

AS: It's not for us to judge others, but I know the feeling of what the old folks say runs from "heart to heart and breast to breast." It comes through the radio....They have an anointing that is immediately felt...songs like "The Potter's House." People don't write like that now....They don't ever have to call my name... [I'm] just another one that God has blessed.

I tell my students that music came from God by the way it's constructed. Think about it! All the music ever written over all the years of time comes from seven notes. Seven is the number for completion. Seven notes. When you play a scale, the eighth note repeats number one.

Eastern music has a quarter tone system. The pentatonic scale is built on whole tones. The Western style of music (diatonic) developed half-tones. There are three types of scales: major scales, minor scales, and chromatic. There are three types of minor scales: the natural minor, melodic minor, and harmonic minor. Three forms of scales—eight times three is twenty-four....

When the Lord got him [Professor Dorsey], nobody and nothing could stand in the way. He has a plan for each one. He had a very special plan for Professor Dorsey: for him to expand the Word past people's perception. Repentance is the key word. We come first to praise and worship God for all that He has, is, and will be for us. He is coming again. Every day we see it more and more....

KK: Do you think we'll ever go back to the old traditional music so that the younger generation can hear it?

AS: Oh, they're already going back. They're going back to that hymnbook.

KK: Do you believe that Levitical families still exist in the present day?

AS: I'm a Levite. I am a modern-day Levite. The Levites were those who took care of the temple. They did all the work around the church. They were the musicians, the preachers, the singers. That's all they did. That's all I do. That runs in my family... preachers and musicians.

Music Director Joseph and Pastor Deborah Smith

(Personal Interview, July, 2014)

Joseph Smith [JS] is a son of Pilgrim Baptist Church and is known for his skills and gifts in music ministry. He is a member of many musical organizations, both locally and nationally. He is renowned for his direction of DuBois's oratorio, "The Seven Last Words of Christ," Burleigh's cantata "Born to Die," and other sacred works. His wife, Deborah, pastors the Greater Victory Christian Fellowship Church. Those who knew Thomas A. Dorsey intimately were invited to their home for an interview with the author. They included Junette Alfreda Smith, Dorothy Hill, Mazie Robinson, and Curtis Boyd.

Junette Alfreda Smith [JAS] is the daughter of Julia Mae Smith Whitfield. She was a prodigy who taught adults piano lessons as a child. She is also the organist for Liberty Baptist Church in Chicago and organist for "Truth Speaks," a weekly radio broadcast of the A.R. Leak Funeral Homes in Chicago. She grew up in Pilgrim Baptist Church. Her mother was the pianist for the gospel choir at Pilgrim under Thomas Dorsey, a singer in the group The Celestial Trio, and highly sought after soloist. She also served as Thomas Dorsey's assistant and as the financial secretary for The National Convention of Gospel Choirs and Choruses.

Dorothy Hill [DH] is the daughter of Junette Alfreda Smith. She inherited her grandmother's talents as a singer. She is a recent graduate of St. Xavier College (2012), with a degree in music performance with an emphasis on Voice. Hill is pursuing a master's degree in vocal pedagogy at Northeastern University. She is the director of the Youth Choir at the Liberty Baptist Church in Chicago.

Mazie Robinson [MR] is a well-known gospel singer in the Chicagoland area. She has sung with the renowned Thompson Community

Singers, the St. Stephen Gospel Choir, Chandler Christian Chorale, and the Burke Family Choir. She currently sings with the Allen CME Choir; the Mather Community Chorus, and is the praise team leader for the Christian Methodist Episcopal Church's third regional conference.

Curtis Boyd [CB] was a former Pilgrim choir member and singer. He directed under the guidance and leadership of Dr. Dorsey and, with Dr. Dorsey, was a member of the 1960s group, The Haloes. He was also Dorsey's roommate on many convention trips.

CB: I got my training as far as voice is concerned from the Chicago Music College and the Chicago Metropolitan School of Music. My teacher, Mrs. "B," was very interested in me, my future, and my voice. I was very fond of Nat King Cole when I started out. I imitated him for one of my class performances. Mrs." B" stopped me in the middle of the song and said, "Curtis, No! You will never make it by imitating anyone else. Get your own style." She taught me a great deal about speaking, diction. It really helped me a lot. Mr. Dorsey also helped me. He taught me some things I will never forget: how to hold my breath and how to follow leads. "Sing the song with feeling" [imitating Dr. Dorsey]. Not only with feeling, but also with me realizing that diction was very important. "Pronounce your words, [he would say]."

KK: He wanted you to enunciate well.

CB: One thing I loved about him and will never forget. He wanted-to see you utilize your talents. [Imitating Mr. Dorsey] "Now son, do you know music"?

"Yes, sir."

"Well, I want you to make sure now that you know what you're doing." I appreciated that. He was to me not a selfish man. He shared his gift of God. I learned that he was a loving and kind man. I learned so much about that man. I recall on many occasions when we were in the room together we would sit and talk. He shared with me how God had touched him…and that he became bitter with God for taking his wife….

(Boyd shares information about his music ministry.)

CB: I'm going to boast a little now. I've been blessed by God so that He's used me throughout the years. I've inspired and uplifted others' spirits as well as my own. When I sing, I want to make sure I feel it, and I want to pass it on to others, too. I put myself in it. I didn't really understand how much I had touched people until I got older.

KK: Were you born in Chicago?

CB: No, I was raised in Chicago. It is home. My family is from Arkansas.

KK: When did you come to Pilgrim?

CB: I was in the streets singing ballads. I was a club singer. I enjoyed that, but it wasn't like what I encountered when I really got in the choir. I respected him [Dorsey] and learned a lot from him. I started traveling with him in the 1950s to the convention.

KK: Was that the National Baptist Convention?

JS: No, no. That was his convention. He only attended the National Baptist Convention when it met at Pilgrim.

CB: It was the National Convention of Gospel Choirs and Choruses. A lot of your organizations and churches as a whole wanted to be a part of Mr. Dorsey's convention. He was the draw. By him having that convention, a lot of your big ministers wanted to be a part of that. Consequently, they rallied about him—a lot of the big preachers. In fact, When Rev. Austin heard Professor Dorsey way, way, back [then], he wanted him—he wanted some of that.

KK: He took him from Ebenezer. Now, I know gospel music started at Ebenezer. "Say Amen Somebody" says it started at Pilgrim.

JAS: Austin encouraged him [Dorsey] and allowed him to do what he did.

KK: He couldn't do that at Ebenezer?

JAS: I don't think so.

CB: Speaking of Frye, he and Professor Frye were tight. They were good friends. They were very close. A lot of people back in the day frowned on that type of music. Many church folks were "seditty." They were too dignified.

JAS: He played like [thumping her hands on the table]. I loved to hear him play.

KK: It was like the juke joint.

CB: His wife [first wife Nettie] tried to get him to come over way before he did, but he was used to this [the secular venues]. This was where the money was. A lot of people shunned that type of music. "Gospel music? What are you talking about! No, we don't want this." But eventually—just to show you how God works—it was the thing.

KK: Blacks just migrating from the South wanted music that they could relate to. They couldn't relate to the anthems and spirituals [arranged spirituals]. Some people nickname gospel "the sacred sister to the blues."

JS: Do you have a copy of all six verses of "Precious Lord"?

JAS: I think there were six verses. Marabeth Gentry would know. Her father and Mr. Dorsey were tight. Do you remember the ladies who came? Marabeth's mother and that other little lady from St. Louis used to come every year with Rev. Gore to the revivals. She was the president of the St. Louis Gospel Choral Union.

CB: Yes. They were part of the convention.

JS: There was a little lady who had a physical defect on her back. How would you describe her range? She would just go up and up and never stop. You know what I'm talking about Curtis.

CB: Yes, yes.

JS: Mr. Gaines, the saw man. He would play "Precious Lord" on a [crosscut] saw. The regular saw like you had at your house.

JAS: I've got a picture of Mr. Gaines. Mama used to play for him.

JS: He'd bend that saw back and play "Precious Lord" and other Dorsey songs.

JAS: He played it with a violin bow string—a crosscut saw.

KK: You're saying there was a revival at Pilgrim every year and these ladies from St. Louis would come with Rev. Gore?

JAS: Yes. The lady you were talking about....They had a group, and they used to come every year and sing. They used to tear it up. Her mother [Geneva Gentry] and another little lady....

JAS: Now her Mama [Junette's mother, Julia Mae Smith] could go up there. Take this lady [St. Louis Choral President] and multiply it by two. She could go up there. We'd just be sitting there waiting....

CB: Those were the days. If you could have heard her mother [Julia Smith] sing. There was one song of Mr. Dorsey's that she used to sing "When I've Done the Best I Can." Her mother could do a job on that.

JAS: Did you ever hear my mother sing "He Doeth All Things Well"? (She hummed a little of it). It's on one of the Sallie Martin albums. Outstanding!

JS: You need to get the music, and we need to reconvene.

JAS: Mr. Dorsey nicknamed me "Gospella" when my mother was carrying me.

KK: Do you sing?

JAS: Just in the choir.

KK: You passed it on to your daughter?

JAS: Yeah, she got it…. I had every book of Mr. Dorsey's and practically every piece of music he ever wrote. I even had some of his original manuscripts. I kept some for myself. I gave a lot of them to Mrs. Dorsey. I still have a number of Sallie Martin's albums. My mother used to work at Martin & Morris.

KK: You had a goldmine.

CB: This is one of his originals (shares a Dorsey song on sheet music entitled "Forgive Me Lord and Try Me One More Time."

KK: Do you remember Magnolia Lewis Butts?

CB: Yes, yes. You can't forget her.

JAS: Do you know who else was a part of our convention? Ramsey Lewis's father was a part of the convention. His sisters, too. I have a picture of all the young people and his two sisters are in that picture with my mother. The Celestial Trio was the supervisor [the adult mentor(s) responsible for a group of youth at the Dorsey Convention].

(Junette then tells of a picture taken at the Singer's Home [home established by Thomas Dorsey and Sallie Martin for older singers).

JAS: Do you remember Mrs. Hampton?

CB: Yes.

JAS: Mrs. Hampton's daughter Bernadine? She and I took a picture. It was on an Easter's Sunday at the Singers' Home at 4048 Lake Park on those stairs—together. My mother submitted my picture to the *Chicago Tribune*, and it won. The prize was $25.00.

KK: That was big money.

JAS: Right—in 1955—yes.

CB: Mr. Dorsey's sister lived in that building.

JAS: My play grandmother lived there, too. So, I was over there all the time. That was my second home.

KK: Were you there when James Cleveland left the Dorsey convention? Around 1968?

JS: Didn't he belong to Pilgrim?

KK: He used to come to Pilgrim as a child with his grandmother. Dr. Dorsey made a platform for him and wrote a song for him. He sang his first song at Pilgrim at the age of eight.

JS: I thought I heard something about him being at Pilgrim.

CB: I didn't really know him until later when he got famous.

JAS: I was a little kid. I remember him vaguely. I was a part of the youth department—my growing up years. That was fun. We learned a lot of music. We sang on Friday nights. We had a humongous crowd.

CB: Do you recall when Pilgrim and Dr. Dorsey used to go to the church [Liberty Baptist Church] you play for?

JAS: Vaguely. The choir I came to play for here [was] the Sanctuary Choir. I used to go to their concerts. Now, we don't have a sanctuary choir. They merged it.

(The interviewees then began to discuss choirs, directors, musicians, and programs throughout the years in Chicago.)

CB: What's the gentleman's name who was close to Dr. Dorsey? We used to go over there all the time. I can't think of his name. They were very, very close.

JAS: Dr. Tamberlin Thomas from Liberty.

CB: Let me give you guys a little humor about Mr. Dorsey that re- ally fascinated me. We went to Washington, D.C., to a con-

136

vention. The people were really cutting up [shouting and praising God in the devotion service] before he [Mr. Dorsey] came in the sanctuary. The people were having a good time, jumping all over the place. I thought they had the spirit. This was before he came in to give his annual speech.

Mr. Dorsey saw what was going on. He walked up on the podium and said "Okay, that's enough now. Let's get quiet now." He shut it down. The spirit just went out. I wonder now if it really was the spirit because a person [he's not God] can't shut it down just like that.

JAS: Do you remember those consecrations we used to have? Everyone was in white.

CB: Willie Mae Ford Smith was over it. She could really sing. A lot of the people back in the day could really sing back then. Willie Mae Ford, Sallie Martin, Mahalia Jackson, the Barrett Sisters. Your mother was the queen of the convention, and even Marabeth Gentry....

JAS: Mrs. Dorsey was very adamant about disassociating herself from the convention.   Something happened that she didn't like.

JS: How long ago was that?

JAS: About twenty years ago, but she still supported Pilgrim.

KK: Do you know how or why they lost the singers' building?

JS: I don't know anything about it.

JAS: The building was really very old. It was a mansion, but it was a frame building. I thought they just got the money from HUD to build a new singers' building. There's an apartment building on it now. (A high rise has now been built at that location).

JS: But they don't own it?

JAS: No. I've still got pictures of it. My mother has baby pictures of me there.

CB: I remember Mr. Dorsey always said that "if you can talk, you can sing."

MR: I'll always remember him directing with that one finger.

PS: I remember going to a concert at Pilgrim. Mr. Dorsey was up in age and couldn't sing. He whistled the melody of the song. It was beautiful. Dr. Dorsey [whistling] was like a bird. I told my husband whistling is an outside thing unless you're Dr. Dorsey. He is the only one who can whistle in the house.

(The discussion moved to the changes in gospel music that began with the rise in popularity of contralto voices.)

MR: High soprano soloists were being replaced by altos like Mahalia Jackson, Albertina Walker, and Shirley Caesar.

(Junette Smith recalls details concerning Ramsey Lewis Jr.)

JAS: Ramsey Lewis Jr. attended the convention also in his youth. He was awarded a music scholarship by the convention.

Pastor Rodney A. Teal, Esq.

(Personal Interview, April, 2014)

Rev. Teal is a modern-day Levite, known throughout the nation as a theologian, biblical teacher, evangelist, pastor, singer, and composer. He holds degrees from the Howard University School of Divinity (in Theology and Theological Studies, and a Master's of Divinity) and from Washington & Lee University (Doctor of Jurisprudence). Teal pastors the historic Jerusalem Baptist Church in the Georgetown area of Washington, D.C. At the same time, he serves the GMWA (the Gospel Music Workshop of America) as an advisory board member, instructor, and songwriter. Dr. Teal states that "His passion is preaching—from pulpit, choir stand, or lecture podium—trumpeting the Word of the Lord with power, clarity, and integrity."

KK: How does prophecy inform music?

RT: 1 Chronicles, Chapter 25, defines ministry as prophecy set to music…[it] is a guiding principle that shapes the way in which I view music and its role in the church….It's not really designed to be music—it's designed to be prophecy that is accompanied by music. Music accompanies prophecy…the music isn't the principal vehicle…doesn't contain the Word of God—the prophecy does…how prophecy functions….Paul says in 1 Cor. 14. that prophecy speaks to others for their exhortation, edification, and comfort….Music in the church ought to be speaking the Word of God to the people of God for purposes of edifying, exhorting them, and comforting them, and that's a different thing from the Gospel Top 40... radio air play...the point is whether or not it is the Word of God shared with the people of God.

KK: Do you see the prophetic message more in the music of the early songwriters, such as Thomas Dorsey, Roberta Martin, and James Cleveland?

RT: ...In the early years of gospel, Rev. Dorsey and others...there was a greater attempt to remain true to speaking the Word of God for exhortation, edification, and comfort in ways that are not necessarily predominant now because gospel has become an industry in which the goal is to sell records.... it is the thing...you're not selling the record because of prophecy...what is the theology and prophecy in some of these songs? How do these songs edify and exhort the body? How does it comfort us....Is that what the Bible teaches? What becomes popular and sung in our churches is driven in large numbers by radio play...a tune and a catchy rhyme. Do they use the Word of God for the edification of God's people? What is their doctrinal use for substantive prophecy?

KK: Does the gospel music we hear in the church today now actually minister to the people?

RT: There is a problem with some of the music. I don't think there is a problem with all of the music...part of our challenge is to distinguish between the sacred and the common, the holy and the unholy...we have not done the work we ought to do in terms of evaluating the music and its appropriateness for worship. Does it do what music is supposed to do? Is this the vehicle for sharing the Word of God for the people of God, or do we just want to have good music?

KK: Do you see the pastor today in the same position as the Levitical priest in the Old Testament to make sure that the service… edifies the people and glorifies and exalts God?

RT: I do, and I think that aiding the pastor in that effort is people with musical knowledge, being a pastor… a cooperative effort to be carried out by both pastor and musical staff.

KK: Are our children who have grown up in church seeing prophecy and theology of music, as something that leads to Christ, or are they just seeing music as an activity to be involved in, something to do?

RT: I think we have done them a disservice….We don't teach music ministry to children; we just teach them about singing, and, in too many instances, the people who are teaching them about singing are not concerned about the lyrics they are singing. They just want them to sing something the children want to sing…they like it because they heard it on the radio, but that doesn't mean it's appropriate for worship.

KK: What can we do, in your estimation, to make music ministry prophetic and real again for our children and young adults that will instill the values that were instilled in us and that seem to have been lost, perhaps, in a generational span, or is it incumbent on the gospel artists to change?

RT: I don't think it is incumbent on the gospel artists to change. It doesn't really matter what they do... if we do the right thing in our churches....We allow them too much power....There was an artist whose work I admired for years that I stopped buying....She decided to go with a [secular] producer. This wasn't the type of music I wanted my children exposed to....I wasn't angry, but I stopped buying her music because I know there are producers out there who could do this and more....I really have issues with choosing secular artists to promote a spiritual album. But I also get to choose what I buy.   I think music directors, in consultation with the pastor, have a choice and responsibility in deciding what type of music they will use. Unless your pastor has a music background, he or she really is relying on the music staff to tell him or her what to do....The song has to stand or fall on its own merit...just don't play pieces of the song....I've always been a stickler for lyrics....Words are important. Words convey our thoughts. I need to understand what it is we are trying to say, and what it is we are not saying.

KK: Do you think there is any possibility of churches and conventions bringing back anthems, spirituals, and gospel hymns as a regular part of worship, or do you think the praise and worship teams will make those things passé?

RT: I think that churches that have intelligent, inspired leadership will continue to have anthems, spirituals, and hymns....

Some churches are trend churches…they do what everyone else does because they're in competition…whatever's hot … without necessarily evaluating whether it's right.

Mr. Kenneth Woods

(Personal Interview, February, 2014)

Kenneth Woods, Jr., is well-known in Chicago and throughout the country for his talents and skills in directing and as a musician. He has received many awards for his musical prowess, including one from the NCGCC. He taught music for many years in the Chicago Public School System. He serves as organist for Bethesda Baptist Church, one of the well-known "silk-stocking" churches in Chicago. He has worked with many of the legends in gospel music throughout the years.

KK: You have vast music experience. What was your relationship with Thomas Dorsey?

KW: When I started in gospel music…when I was introduced [to it]—I was fourteen and a freshman at Crispus Attucks High School in Indianapolis, Indiana. I was invited …to a youth group that met at Willie Suggs's house…so I went…September 1943. I was enthralled—I joined; mind you now, at that time, there were no records, CDs, no anything—no one teaching gospel music. There were about three musicians older than I….I would hear them—my ear is quick—I learned to play. And the very next month, October 1943, I was introduced to Beatrice Brown. Beatrice Brown was the national supervisor of the youth department of the Dorsey organization.

KK: I remember hearing her name.

KW: She wrote "Without God, I Could Do Nothing." Her group was called The Brown Inspirational Singers....Let me show you how the spirit works. I had no lessons in teaching how to put notes down on a manuscript...but I was taking piano lessons....Then I started at fifteen years of age arranging Ms. Brown's music for publication. I still have a lot of it at my house... [From Brown's tutelage, Woods learned to play gospel music in different keys: Ab, F, G, and Eb] we weren't doing Gb and Db at that time....

(Woods tells how he was able to influence established singers in Indianapolis to sing with Ms. Brown. They were Melvin Gurkin and Charles Royster, who were already singing with Rev. J.T. Highball.)

KW: In 1945 we went to the convention in Detroit....I remember us going to Pittsburgh and Allentown, Pennsylvania...I remember some of the names: Geneva Gentry and her husband Joshua Gentry—Marabeth wasn't even born at that time.... Kenneth Moales—I met him when I came out of the service along with the O'Neal Twins. We were about the same age. I remember when we went to Detroit in 1945. Nobody stayed in those hotels. We stayed in homes for $2.00 a night.

But then, the big convention was the Dorsey Convention. Somewhere along that time, Theodore Frye tried to organize something from the National Baptist Convention. It really didn't materialize...so the main gospel convention was Mr. Dorsey's...and whenever he [Dorsey] would see me, even if he couldn't remember my name, he [would] always connect me with Ms. Brown.

144

KK: You knew most of the gospel pioneers personally?

KW: I played for Sallie Martin for about twenty years. After she and Kenneth Morris split—Kenneth Morris stayed with the Martin and Morris Studio and Sallie Martin went over there and took out Bowles at 79th and Prairie. So then Kenneth Morris was the arranger and manuscript guy for Martin and Morris at 4312 Indiana—then I began doing it for Ms. Martin at 79th and Prairie.... I was out there one day. Mr. Dorsey came in. He remembered me from Ms. Brown. So I became assistant pianist for the youth department back in the 1940s.

(Woods relates an incident with Bertha Smith.)

KW: Bertha Smith—she was the daughter of Willie Mae Smith. She played for the youth department, and she was hardly a youth... I was a youth because I was a teenager. I was the pianist for Ms. Brown until I went into the service and scored practically everything she published. During that time, I met The Roberta Martin Singers. I met Theodore Frye because he would come down to Ms. Martin's house for convention-related business, [and] Ms. Willie Mae [Smith] came through, of course. When I met Sallie Martin, I was fifteen because I came here from Indianapolis to play for three singers.

Do you remember Emma Jackson? She was a powerhouse in the 1940s and 1950s. Her studio was somewhere in the 1940s and 1950s on Indiana. Ms. Martin came in. She was about 48. She began to associate me with Beatrice Brown. Somewhere around that time, I met James Cleveland who played for The Lux Singers—oh, they were some singing folks .... All the music back then was so much better than it is now—and the gospel music way back—1930s, 1940s, 1950s—all the way to 1968—because it was here [points to his heart] spirit-filled… but now it's all amplified.…Now it's the same thing all over again.…In 1968—that was the year that Edwin Hawkins came out with the new sound and different chord progressions— a whole lot of Db and Gb, and everything has changed, and with their progeny, everything has changed even more.…But I'm from the old school. I remember all the music from my grandmother in the 1930s.…all the music around that time was built around soloists.

(Woods relates how music was demonstrated by Thomas Dorsey's singers.)

KW: Mr. Dorsey had these ladies who sang with him in the middle 1930s. Ms. Armstrong, Ms. Brown, and Ms. Martin traveled with Mr. Dorsey to Los Angeles around 1937.…Something happened around that time.…Sallie Martin made her name with Mr. Dorsey. Mr. Dorsey and Sallie parted ways in 1939… and then the next year she and Kenneth Morris formed a new music concern, thanks to Rev. Clarence H. Cobbs.… She was at First Church of Deliverance, even though she was a member of Pilgrim. They hooked up and formed his little business alliance in 1940. Their first big hit was "Just a Closer Walk with Thee." The young people don't know anything about that.…

(Woods remembers that Thomas Dorsey worked in both the sacred and secular music arenas. He remembers his songs being simultaneously in the *Gospel Pearls* and blues venues.)

146

KW: But when Mr. Dorsey was coming out of the blues world, about 1929, he had a big hit "Oh, It's Tight Like That"…but when he finally came out….He wrote a piece about 1921 or 1922 that was in the *Gospel Pearls*.

(Woods recalled the first marriage, death of wife and son, and "Precious Lord" as well as this new sound of gospel music; the friendship between Thomas Dorsey and Theodore Frye and the choir they started at Ebenezer).

KK: There is still some controversy about where gospel music started. The pastor of Pilgrim says it started there.

KW: It did start at Ebenezer, though. This is why you have to be so sure about facts because facts can be so distorted, you know, that people think they're real.

(Mr. Woods told about a Dorsey convention he attended. He went to a workshop where the teacher—a lady from St. Louis—in a history class, stated that gospel music began at Pilgrim. He told her his name, Kenneth Woods, and that gospel music first started at Ebenezer).

KW: They had a song they created that was so popular—I think it was "I'm on the Battlefield"…they had an invitation to go to Pilgrim…I think they had to sit in the balcony because the big choir was the Sanctuary Choir…with their anthems, they were popular…some of them were so high class [that] they disassociated themselves from the music of the South….but Rev. Austin liked it… [he said] how about that over here at Pilgrim? Now, at Ebenezer there was Dorsey on the piano and Frye conducting and also singing….Now, when Rev. Austin got Dorsey at Pilgrim, then Frye got Roberta Martin out of

Morgan Park at Ebenezer, and that's where she stayed many years—and that's how it was.

KK: I'm mortified that I've known you for years and never really knew your deep, deep roots in gospel music...You're one of the last few people who really knew the greats.

KW: All of the other greats...are gone...when I was sixteen, the Dorsey convention was at the Church of Our Faith in Detroit on Columbia [Avenue]. That August of 1945, I was standing outside, and up drives Roberta Martin in this beautiful convertible with The Roberta Martin Singers—Delois Barrett, Willie Webb, and Eugene Smith....but you know—we didn't come to stay....

KK: What do you think of the trend of the gospel music today? The performance and the secular platform?

KW: That's exactly where it is [touching the heart]. You can tell the difference...what goes from heart to heart....Young people don't know anything about that—anything before 1968. They call it their grandmother's music, and that's where the source of all spirituality is....Now we have emulated the white people with praise and worship—singing the same thing over and over again.

KK: Is there anything that can be done right now to bring gospel musicians back to the throne room....I'm speaking specifically about the singers. What can we do so that their singing will be consecrated to such a level that it transforms the lives of a lot of people....because as a people, we have lost touch with the music—and that's what made us whole....

KW: That's the purpose of conventions, because before Dorsey, there was the National Baptist Convention. It split, and split again, but even with the split, there was still a certain type of music that was prevalent and popular from around 1890—until Lucie Campbell's "Something within Me".... Lucie Campbell was a powerhouse. You know those songs.... Some time ago, I had a young girl, a dramatist at Bethesda read the words....We sing a lot of hymns at Bethesda....There has to be a turnaround....there's nothing better than a cappella singing....I had to play an organ solo—"Amazing Grace." It went quite well...the next time I was asked....I brought everyone in—and then I stopped [playing].

(At age 85, Woods no longer participates in music conventions. The people he knew, played, and scored music for are all gone. His later years were spent teaching many students how to sing. He continues to perform annual concerts at Bethesda including "Born to Die," where he trains many in worship and singing unto the Lord. He appreciates the many years he had in gospel music with gratitude. His advice to the younger musicians is to "go back another way, more a cappella music...and learn to read music").

KW: Many of the greats came from Chicago—Chicago was on the map.

Rev. Dr. Jeremiah A. Wright, Jr.
(Personal Interview, August, 2014)

The Rev. Dr. Jeremiah A. Wright, Jr. is an eminent theologian and

Pastor Emeritus of Trinity United Church of Christ in Chicago. He is also a lecturer, author, scholar, composer, social justice activist, educator, musician, and ethnomusicologist. He is perhaps best known nationally as having been the pastor of President Barack Obama when he was a member of Trinity before being elected president. Wright's innumerable achievements and contributions to society have enriched the lives of countless people throughout the years of his ministry and advocacy.

KK: How do you define the genres of sacred and gospel music?

JW: The second chapter of the book *The Universe Bends toward Justice: Radical Reflections on the Bible, the Church, and the Body Politic* is Obery's analysis of gospel music. It is so well written, that I think it would help you for what you're trying to capture. Obery is showing—in terms of gospel music—how gospel music that grew out of the African American religious experience has shifted from the notions of "we" and "us" and "our" to "me." It has gotten so narcissistic and self-centered that it's no longer music that would inspire our people. It's all about me. "Take Me to the Throne," "I Got Favor"—meaning material things—"God Favors Me," "Increase My Territory." It's not what it used to be—it's entertainment now—not inspirational. If you listen to a lot of the words—the words ain't got nothing to do with Jesus of Nazareth—the way which we've come, and the way which our people have come. The music that chronicles that story has changed. Our children don't know those old songs—our kids don't know the origins. They don't know the roots.

KK: We have a generation of musicians and singers who don't know our history.

JW: The youngest lot of our musicians—Bryan Johnson is a happy
        exception—but he learned from Jeffrey Radford and Bobby
        Wooten (former ministers of music at Trinity United Church
        of Christ). [Bryan Johnson is the Executive Director of Music
        at Trinity United Church of Christ]. They [younger musicians]
        not only don't know the gospel tradition—they don't know
        hymns.

(Wright describes the qualifications for a minister of music at a church
that values the totality of the African American worship experience.)

JW: A part of their job description would be not only to know, but
        to teach anthems, spirituals, gospel, traditional gospel, con-
        temporary gospel, Afro-Caribbean, and African music be-
        cause of the wide spectrum of worshippers who gather on a
        Sunday from all of those various traditions. I think to lose any
        part of that is to lose a part of our heritage—including com-
        mon meter, long meter, and short meter. So many of our
        young people do not know meter singing.

(He related an experience involving students from Paul Quinn College at Dr. Frederick Haynes Church—Friendship West Baptist Church
in Dallas, Texas—in which young people showed musical knowledge
lost to many of their generation. The assistant director of music, Jewell
Kelly, is a nationally known musician and teacher of African-American music.)

JW: He [Freddie Haynes] had students from Paul Quinn College
        singing behind me....They blew me out of the water. So many
        of our young people do not know music....I was talking about
        things that get lost in our music tradition....I started singing
        "I Love the Lord; He Heard My Cry." The kids in the choir

behind me picked it up. They said: "Oh yeah; we know it."…
If the teachers don't teach it, it gets lost. They don't do that
kind of singing in the mega churches. They do it in the rural areas and in some small storefronts.…so a kid growing up
in the mega church never heard it… and forget about the rich
heritage of shape notes. They don't know what that is—not
because they're stupid—but because no one ever taught it to
them. If we don't pass it on and teach our kids, the tradition
dies with us when we die.

(He shares an experience that occurred during a live recording at
Trinity Church when the musician couldn't read music and didn't
know hymns).

JW: Live recording…V. Michael McKay wrote half of the songs on
        that CD. The end of one of Michael's songs, "Oh Lord Bless
        Me," is Hallelujah, Oh Lamb of God I come" (three times).
        Michael jumps up and runs into the choir room and pushes
        Jeffrey aside (so he could direct the song). While they [the
        choir] are holding come …he [Michael] said to the musician
        [who had never heard the song]: " 'Just as Am without One
        Plea,' same key." He grew up in Milton Brunson's church.…
        Ted Brewer (Trinity bassist, degreed in music, with musical
        knowledge and skills) puts the hymn book in front of him.…
        Jeffrey bumps him off the piano and begins playing "Just as I
        Am…" because the [musician who was playing] didn't read
        music. Unrehearsed, V. Michael McKay led us into "Just as I
        Am without One Plea."

KK: That's a real concern now with musicians and praise teams.

JW: They don't know the hymns. They don't know Charles Albert Tindley, Lucie Campbell. They don't know their black hymnodists before you even get to the twentieth century. They came before Dorsey, Roberta Martin, and Sallie Martin. It starts for them with Andrae Crouch, Walter Hawkins, and Tramaine Hawkins…modern contemporary gospel sound—that's all they know.

KK: "Oh Happy Day" starts it.

JW: Some of them don't go back that far. Tramaine Hawkins's "A Change Has Come Over Me"; Andrae Crouch's "I Don't Know Why Jesus Loves Me"—that's as far back as they go.

(Wright relates a special service he attended in Minneapolis, Minnesota. The musician, Leo White surprised him by playing a song he had composed).

JW: He just blessed me in a special way. I was in Minneapolis for the installation of Barbara Holmes, who was to become the first black female president of the United Theological Seminary in Minneapolis-St. Paul. Barbara asked me to introduce Renita Weems, who would give the installation message. We've got our heads bowed in prayer during the invocation. (Leo White had been asked to be the guest musician). I'm listening to this song he was playing. I said to Renita, "That's my song. He's playing a song I wrote." (Leo White, a gifted musician, originally from Chicago, had learned that song from Jeffrey Radford, the former minister of music at Trinity United Church of Christ while Rev. Wright was Senior Pastor).

153

KK: What was the name of the song?

JW: "Jesus Is His Name." Charles Clency did it in his concert. (Dr.
        Charles Clency is a well-known music professor, musician,
        choral director, and composer, who was the pianist and ar-
        ranger for Mahalia Jackson).

(Wright segues into the next part of the question, sharing his experiences of cataloguing music for his professor at Howard University.)

JW: In the 1968 to 1969 academic year, I became John Lavelle's
        teaching assistant. I had to catalog all the music. It was there
        that I found out that black sacred music, the definition, is
        much larger and wider than I had thought it was. For Africans,
        the line of demarcation between sacred and secular is nonex-
        istent. This used to upset some of the white slave preachers
        because what they heard on Sunday morning sounded ex-
        actly like what they heard Saturday night.

        Our music uses percussion; our music uses beats. Bishop
        Daniel Alexander Payne and Absalom Jones were dragged out
        of St. George's Methodist Episcopal Church in Philadelphia.
        Alexander Payne kept the European music in his church ser-
        vice and added an A (African) in front of M.E (Methodist Epis-
        copal). Absalom Jones went into the Anglican Church. You
        must remember that worship in Philadelphia and New York
        was very, very British. Same worship, same liturgy.

        Methodist music changed when it came past Baltimore and
        into Virginia, North Carolina, and South Carolina. When it

154

got to the Low Countries, the Gullahs and Geechees brought their African rhythms, their African drums, their banjoes, their tambourines, and washboards. Bishop Payne hated black music. He was trained at the Lutheran School of Theology. In fact, when he went to [worship service at] Charleston, South Carolina, he told the presiding elder, "We've got to stomp out this fist and heel music." The presiding elder said something very profound to him concerning sacred music for Africans: "Without the beat the spirit don't come."

When you look in the Scriptures, it's right there in front of your face: Psalm 100, Psalm 150: Miriam grabbed her tambourines…they are percussive. 1 Samuel: 19 is even heavier. King Saul is chasing David to kill him. David is running for his life. He ran to Samuel's seminary—the training school for prophets. How do they get happy?

KK: Through the music?

JW: Through exotic dance. Exuberant, exotic, exciting dance. When you get happy, the spirit takes over and you can prophesy. Remember what happened in Second Kings, third chapter? Jehoshaphat said, "I need a prophet—get me a prophet"…. The prophet asked for a musician. "Get me a musician—bring me a musician." As soon as the musician began to play, the spirit came in. That's sacred music. African traditional music—African sacred music—is the same. The body is not dirty—the body is sacred. Have you ever been to Nigeria?

KK: No.

JW: You see moves like you see on BET and MTV—right there in
        church. To them, the body is not dirty. The body is sacred, and
        the body gets involved in the movements. Europeans taught
        us that it's [the body's] not sacred.

(He talks about the difference in worship among African-Americans
in America and among people of African descent in the Caribbean
and South America).

JW: I began to see by studying with Lavelle that the African
        understanding of sacred music and our understanding of
        sacred music—is very different from the European under-
        standing. When you go to Brazil, Haiti, Trinidad, and Tobago,
        you see drums and music that weren't allowed in the United
        States. They were Catholic. They let the Africans keep their
        drums.

        Drums weren't allowed in America. Drums were frightening
        to Europeans—not only because of the percussiveness and
        the sensuousness of those beats, but because they could com-
        municate with each other across language groupings and lin-
        guistic groupings. The Europeans didn't understand what
        they were saying or communicating, so they outlawed it in
        the United States of America.

        In terms of sacred music—you remember Wyatt T. Walker's
        work? There's more than one genre—more than just the spiri-
        tuals, more than the slave seculars, the field hollers, and the
        communal folk nature. We need courses in seminary on mu-

sic. So many people graduate, and they don't have a clue on how music and worship go together. DuBois said it in 1903, "there are three elements in black worship: the music, the preaching, and the Holy Spirit. Take any one of them away and you have a club, a social club, a civic club, not a church." (Wright addresses the relationship between the pastor and the music staff).

JW: A lot of preachers get threatened by the music. The music is essential. The music ushers in the spirit. It makes preaching easy. Stop fighting with the musicians. Work together as a team.

Spirituals are folk music. Spirituals are folk literature. They come from the people. They have no authors that you can put a name on. When you see a name attached to a spiritual, it denotes the arrangement of the spiritual. John Work, Rosalind Johnson, James Weldon Johnson, Roland Carter—those are arrangements from folk music. Folk music from different parts of the country uses different tunes, but it comes out of the folk and it's pulled together like the Books of Moses.

That communal folk creation of spirituals that led into the gospel music of Dorsey, Roberta Martin (and others) from that era…there was a "we" ness about them. "We've Come This Far by Faith, Leaning on the Lord." That kind of "we" of communal creation has changed, in my perception of it, for the worse because it has taken the focus off of us as a community, and we have become self-centered. African people are communal.

157

(Wright then introduces the "7-11 Praise" sermon that he preached).

JW: I just preached about that a few Sundays ago. Do you know what the "7-11 Praise" is?

KK: I'm not sure. Seven stanzas said several times?

JW: No. [It's] seven words sung eleven times: "Come on everybody, let's praise the Lord." Can we say it again (over and over again)? It's that type of desire for popularity by singing what you've heard on the radio....

KK: I've heard that before.

JW: Do you know how the Holiness Church got started? Cheryl Townsend Jelks helped me understand that.

KK: It came out of the Methodist church.

JW: Yeah, because the Methodists were singing the songs wrong. (Wright then illustrates the different tempo in which the hymn "What a Fellowship" is sung by Methodists and Holiness congregations).

JW: That whole story of how our young people got lost because they never knew the history of the hymns. How often do you consider the words of the song, "When I Survey the Wondrous Cross" (He recites the words.)? Words like that get lost in four beats of the same two phrases [sung] over and over again. On the black side—the prince of the pulpit—Charles

Albert Tindley—not his first verse—his second verse. (He recites the second verse of "We'll Understand It Better Bye and Bye"). Words like that are lost to contemporary gospel music. Even if you take a hymn and put a gospel beat to it…Just look at the words to those hymns that are lost in terms of today's composers of contemporary gospel music…. That troubles me tremendously.

KK: You have given me a definition of sacred music that encompasses everything from our African heritage, to the communal nature, to the folk nature that has been lost with the contemporary music and the narcissistic view of "me" and not "us." Until we get that back, we will have lost the power of our music?

JW: Yes, and also we will have lost the meaning of the faith we share, which is a communal faith.

KK: Not with a person.

JW: God makes faith with a community. Not with an individual. Even when God was talking to Abraham, it was about a community: "through you all nations will be blessed." It's not just you and me. The covenant on Mt. Sinai was with a community: "A new commandment give I unto you that you would love one another as I have loved you." This was for community. It has shifted from community to autonomy. We are losing the meaning of the Gospel of Jesus Christ. For God so loved Thelma—and Thelma only? It's the world we are talking about. A communal faith—we lose it—is my premise.

(Rev. Wright then expounds on what he sees as a problem in the contemporary church—illuminated by a conversation with his grandson, a master's degree candidate in sacred music at Yale University—regarding the contemporary gospel's focus on abortion rights and gay bashing).

JW: With the focus on sexual sins instead of the grace of God and all the things we talk about as a people and all of the struggles we have come through, it's [that focus is] disturbing to me in terms of the contemporary church and its understanding of worship.

The Brown Inspirational Singers. On piano: Kenneth Woods; *Standing left to right:* Milan Brown, Beatrice Brown, Raymond Raspberry, Delorese (Della) Reese. (Courtesy of Kenneth Woods.)

Cummings Family Banner commemorating five generations of participation in the National Convention of Gospel Choirs and Choruses (Courtesy of Michael Cummings.)

The Thomas Dorsey Bandstand, Villa Rica, Georgia. *From left*: Councilwoman Shirley Marchman, President, Dorsey Birthplace Choir; Eric Ayers, Minister of Music, Dorsey Birthplace Choir.

The Halo Singers. *Standing left to right:* Willie Mae Hampton, Gertrude Allen, Mary Gloster, (unidentified), Curtis Boyd, and Thomas A. Dorsey at piano. (Courtesy of Curtis Boyd.)

The Celestial Trio. *From left to right*: Julia Mae Smith, Marion Peebles, and Willie Ruffin. (Courtesy of Rev. Morris and Dr. Eva Purnell.)

The Ebenezer Gospel Choir. (Courtesy of Ebenezer Baptist Church.)

The braced exterior walls of the historic Pilgrim Baptist Church after a roofing repair fire destroyed the structure in January 2006.

Pilgrim Baptist Church's current location since the destruction of the original edifice.

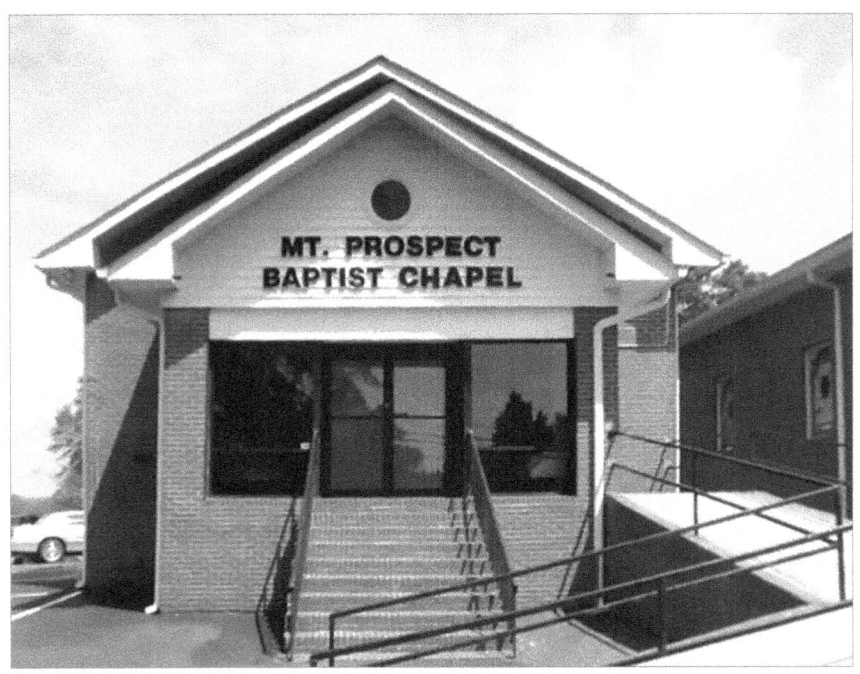

Mt. Prospect Baptist Chapel, Villa Rica, Georgia, where the Dorsey family worshipped.

Rev. James Potts, Pastor of Mt. Prospect Baptist Chapel, Villa Rica, Georgia. (Courtesy of Mt. Prospect Baptist Chapel.)

Thomas Dorsey Drive, Villa Rica, Georgia

The Sallie Martin Singers. *From left to right:* Dorothy Simmons, Melva Williams, Sallie Martin, Julia Mae Smith, and Cora Brewster. (Courtesy of Junette Alfreda Smith.)

Thomas A. Dorsey

Musician
1899-1993

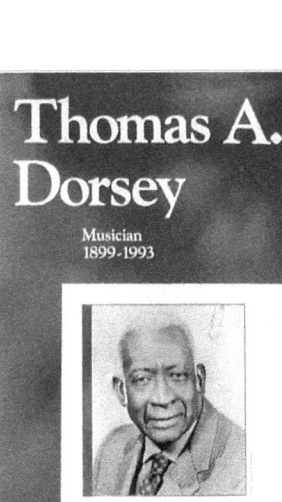

The "father of gospel music," Thomas Dorsey mixed jazz, blues and spirituals to create a new musical genre. Composer, publisher and promoter, he toured the United States with legends Mahalia Jackson and Sallie Martin, bringing gospel music first to black churches and later to the world.

Dorsey moved from Atlanta to Chicago in 1916, and performed as blues pianist "Georgia Tom" during the 1920s. He published a number of popular songs, often with risqué lyrics, and performed with Ma Rainey's blues band.

When Dorsey decided to devote himself to religious music, he took the emotional intensity of the cabaret to the church, composing such works as "Precious Lord, Take My Hand," and "Peace in the Valley." Dorsey's songs were enormously popular—even the leading white gospel publishers were anthologizing his music by 1939.

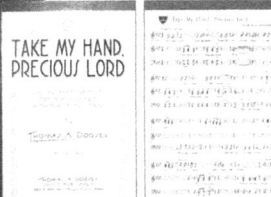

Though gospel was initially controversial within old-line black churches, Dorsey gave it legitimacy after becoming music director at Pilgrim Baptist Church, one of the largest black churches in the U.S., from 1932 to 1983. He and his family spent many of those years here, at 7921 South Indiana Avenue.

Dorsey founded the National Convention of Gospel Choirs and Choruses in 1933, and served as its president for four decades, influencing generations of musicians.

Thomas A. Dorsey Historical
Marker, Chicago Illinois

Ebenezer Missionary Baptist Church

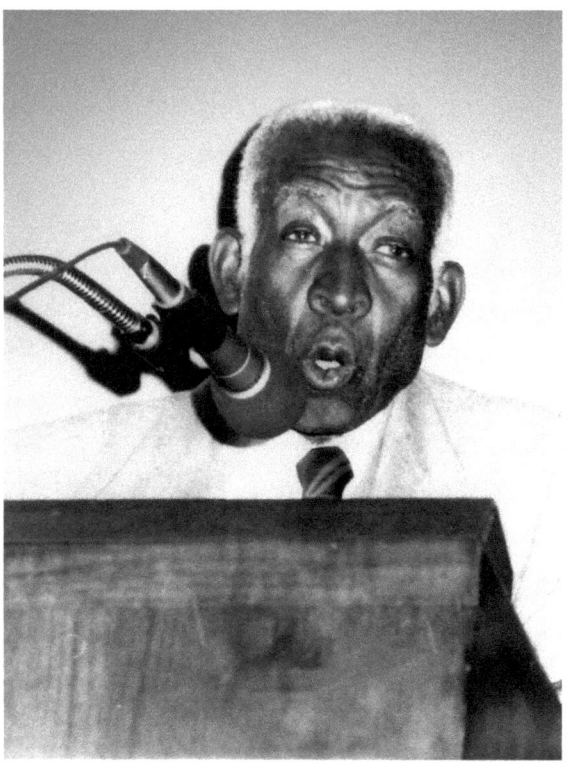

Thomas Dorsey at the mike performing one of his gospel
songs. (Courtesy of his daughter, Doris Dorsey.)

Postscript:

Twenty-first Century Church Worship and Sacred Music

Gospel music has evolved from the early bluesy and jazz chords of the twentieth century to the "Holy" hip hop and rap rhythms of today; thus, historic gospel is father and grandfather to modern and contemporary gospel. (For a chronology of the development of gospel music, see Appendix V). Indeed, secular and sacred, soul and pop, profane and spiritual are all now a part of what is considered "gospel music."

Gospel music belonged to the church from the 1930s through the 1960s. Media exposure was mostly limited to fifteen- to twenty-minute segments on the gospel radio market. One would only find one to three hours of daily programming featuring black formatted radio during that time period. The entrepreneurial black music businesses begun by Dorsey and others that once filled that void are now non-existent—their inventory the property of music corporations.

Changes began to surface in the 1960s when multicultural 24-7, radio, CD, and DVD markets developed. Television, the Internet, and satellite radio now all provide African American gospel content. Increased secular venues such as music festivals, mega concerts, and digital sales in the United States and abroad, have moved gospel music from its original place as church worship music. That desire of gospel artists to appeal to secular interests appears in what is called "Christian music." The selections, however, often insert the

161

word "Jesus" to intimate that it is a gospel song, but the lyrics, in many instances, betray that fact.

Gospel Music as a Moneymaker

Gospel music is a moneymaker for the recording industry. It has grown from a million- to a billion-dollar industry, and today, sacred artists are recording with secular artists, agents, and musicians to such an extent that it has become increasingly difficult to determine whether the music being sung is secular or sacred. This was evidenced recently during the 2015 Grammy Awards when the secular singer, Beyoncé, sung Thomas Dorsey's sacred gospel song, "Precious Lord."

The incident provoked outrage from people throughout the world. Christians were especially outraged by what they termed a "sacrilegious" performance. "Queen Bey" has alter-egos and personas that are antithetical to gospel beliefs. Additionally, questions were raised as to the reasons for her replacement of Ledisi, the artist who performed the song for the movie "Selma," on the Grammys, and who was present during the ceremony.

Beyoncé chose to defend her decision to perform "Precious Lord," stating its rendition was a testament honoring black men and the legacy of her grandparents and father (MUSIC ROUNDUP: Bey Releases B-T-S Look at "Precious Lord"; February 9, 2015). This travesty, nevertheless, underscores the impact of Hollywood and secular interests in determining issues related to public performance of black sacred music.

Gospel as the "Good News"

The question of what constitutes the sacred music genre in the twenty-first century is of profound interest to the author. If gospel is the "good news," the "Godspell," then the music should make that explicit. God is not the "Man Upstairs." God lives in heaven. God isn't your personal commodity. His love is universal. Salvation's message has no gender, ethnicity, or geographical location. God isn't your personal "theological bellhop." He is omnipotent, omnipresent, and omniscient. His arms are big enough to hold the "whole world in His hands." God is a God of action, of justice, and of mercy.

Black worship is viewed through multidimensional lenses in Volume Two of Dr. Abbington's *Readings in African Church Music and Worship* (2014). Worship is examined through an intuitive knowing lens as well as through a rational, objective reality. (See Kemp's Knowledge Construct in Appendix II). Jackson (2004) examines the power of black music from its two knowledge bases. He terms music as "an aural medium... [an] elusive manipulation of time through space. As sound, then, gospel was intractable, fluid, and impervious—properties that allowed it to cross normally impassable racial barriers (Jackson, 134)."

James Baldwin, writer and activist with a Levitical background, also addressed this duality. European Americans view events from a different perspective and core belief than those of African Americans. The son of a clergyman, Baldwin was a storefront preacher as a teenager (Turner, 26). He posited that the use of different lenses was one of the reasons for gospel's broad appeal in the twentieth century. Its full message escaped many people and that, unfortunately, is also true in the twenty-first century for all who view gospel as entertainment and as music that makes you feel good. Baldwin observes that, "It is only in his music, which Americans are able to enjoy because a protective sentimentality limits their understanding of it, that the Negro in America has been able to tell his story (Jackson, 2004, 135)."

Dr. Samuel D. Proctor in *The Theological Validation of Black Worship* (Abbington, 2014) asserts that "Christian worship is the adoration and praise of God and the exercise of seeking communion with God—privately or corporately, in a cathedral or in a tent, in a temple or in an open field, at home or in a store-front (169)." He is concerned about the validity of the religious experience of black people. He terms theology "God-talk" (167), while Dr. Kenneth Ulmer's *Transformational Worship in the Life of a Church*" (Abbington, 2014), defines worship as "interaction with God" (178).

Theologians of the Diaspora know intuitively that black worship and black life are intertwined. Dr. James H. Cone, *in Black Worship: A Historical Theological Interpretation* (Abbington, 2014), speaks of the historical context of black worship as "born in slavery." He emphasizes this connection to our African heritage:

> Black worship was born on the slave ships and nurtured in the cotton fields of Alabama, Arkansas, and Mississippi. African life and culture was the bedrock of the African personality. It was that element in the black slaves' being that structured their response to American slavery and the Christian gospel (154). Black worship…is characterized by a religious sense inseparable from the suffering that determined it …Through sermon, prayer, and song, we transcend societal humiliation and degradation and explore heavenly mysteries about starry crowns and gospel shoes…Apart from the historical reality of oppression and our attempt to liberate ourselves from it, we would have no reason to sing, "My soul looks back and wonders how I got over" (153-154).

Black Theology and Black Worship

Dr. Proctor speaks to Cone's "black theology," which gained national prominence during the Civil Rights Movement. The sermons, songs, and prayers of black people once again spoke of the Jesus who "freed the captives and gave liberty to the blind" (Abbington, 2014). The centrality of "Jesus as Liberator" is also addressed by Wyatt. T. Walker, who emphasizes that:

> Jesus is the central figure in the theology of the contemporary black church. The Jesus faith of blacks reveals an Africanization of Christianity rather than the Christianizing of Africans ....The Jesus faith is covered by its cultural antecedent, traditional West African religion, and is thereby 'holistic' in its theological posture (171).

Black worship has, and always will, address the themes of liberation and deliverance, and, in doing so, will always contain emotional expression, hand-clapping, foot-patting, moans, and shouts. Moreover, it will always be both communal and personal. Gospel music, as music that expresses the totality of the black experience in America, was born from this reality—shaped from this duality. Black worship contains the wisdom and the culture of the West Africans who brought it to America. It will always exist in the aural and oral traditions of people of color. Church music has a sacred duty, and pastoral leaders have the charge to keep the traditions of our musical heritage alive in the twenty-first century.

Blacks, nearly four hundred years later, have a different understanding of worship. We, in the twenty-first century, have lost the theme of a God who liberates. We've forgotten the radical theology practiced by Jesus in Luke 4:18. Too often, we've even dismissed the evangelizing work of the Great Commission in Matthew 28:16-20. To some, there is no difference between white and black worship. To others, black worship must confirm our history and heritage.

Church worship in the twenty-first century faces serious theological issues that it must resolve. Historically, black music and black preaching had addressed the conditions of the African American social reality of that time period. Ante-bellum preachers hummed themes of liberation and deliverance. Post-Reconstruction preachers exhorted their white religious constituents to deal fairly with their newly freed black neighbors and the promises guaranteed by emancipation. Pastors during times of war, the Great Migration, and the Great Depression established social programs and provided economic relief when possible for members of the community.

Despite its shortcomings, Walker, nevertheless still viewed the Black Church as the social institution with the greatest influence in the black community (1979). He states: "Given the black condition in America, the Black Church has a greater potential for a ministry of social change than does any other quarter of black life (185)."

That poses a question for church worship in the twenty-first century. Are churches and pastors interested in worship that feeds the soul and energizes the body for social action, or are they instead more interested in singing songs of praise in the context of pageantry and exhibitions?

The Pastor as Prophet

Black preaching today has lost its prophetic voice. One role of a pastor is as a prophet who preaches about social justice. He or she urges congregants to live the life they sing about in their songs. That includes having the faith to stand up and speak out against laws, decisions, and politics that deny equal freedom to all people. Prophetic preaching demands more than "Amen" and "Praise God." It requires action. "The prophetic critique," states Hendricks, is "principled public criticism of and opposition to systemic injustice (2001, 21)." This is addressed eloquently by the prophet Amos (5:23-24).

Marvin A. McMickle's "When Prophetic Preaching Gives Way to Praise" laments the twenty-first century substitution of praise over prophecy, wherein prophetic preaching is missing in many twenty-first century worship services.

> The burning concerns of prophetic preaching are al-
> most entirely absent. There is a deafening silence on
> such matters as society's care for "the least of these";
> the sovereignty of God over the whole creation and
> not just over America; the lingering problem of rac-
> ism and the festering problem of sexism; the econom-
> ic and human costs of war and the effect that it has
> on domestic programs and many other moral ethi-
> cal demands that are a part of the life of a disciple of
> Christ....If you listen to the sermons on religious tele-
> vision channels, on station after station, day after day,
> one program after another, you will hear this theme of
> praise severed from the prophetic message (Abbing-
> ton, 2014, 327-28).

Black Sacred Music

Gospel composers, singers, and artists also have a black sacred music heritage. This music is based on the norms established by our ancestors who created it. Those norms, evolved from slavery, were expressed in the music of the slaves. The music was collective. It acknowledged the oppression that existed in the lives of the enslaved Africans. There was a prophetic critique in the music, which spoke of consequences and rewards. It spoke to the injustice of slavery. The norms that defined black sacred music have changed. Gospel music has evolved throughout the last century. The gospel train is no longer a locomotive but a bullet train. The legacy of our musical elders [customarily transmitted from generation to generation] was derailed, unknown to the new custodians of gospel music during the twentieth century.

Contemporary Gospel Music

Gospel musicians continually improvise and refine the musical riffs and chords that produce the genre we know as "contemporary gospel music." The irony is that many twenty-first century musicians do not know whom to thank for the foundation that now supports their gifts and talents. Some do not even know who Thomas Dorsey was or about his struggles to revolutionize sacred black worship in churches. They don't know that the implementation of the seventh chord and the special chorus became the trademarks of Dorsey gospel songs.

The genre has changed so much since Edwin Hawkins became the "Father of Contemporary Gospel" that it has become indistinguishable from secular music in many churches. "Holy hip hop" and rap are accepted in many worship services, and there is nothing wrong with those new genres of gospel. They must, however, point to the cross. All praise and worship to God evolves from a biblical perspective. The question of what constitutes praise and worship have a biblical context. How we give praise to God is a reflection of our witness to others. Rodney A. Teal's "Reflections on Praise and Worship from a Biblical Perspective" reiterates the admonition that Dorsey, in the twentieth century, gave his singers. Teal reminds twenty-first century Levites:

> We may witness intentionally or unintentionally. For example, we may intentionally witness to someone by telling them of God's goodness....Further, we may give an unintentional witness by our demeanor, our speech, our lifestyle, etc. This "unintentional, indirect praise" is our walk...How can we do that effectively when our walk does not demonstrate that [we] have drawn water from the wells of salvation...? (Isaiah 12:3) (Abbington, 548).

A Disconnect Between Pastors and Church Musicians

Children and adults born after the Civil Rights Movement, commonly referred to as "Generation X" and the "Millennial Generation," rarely know songs from the historic, classical, or golden ages of gospel. Too many of today's musicians no longer read music. Hymnbooks? They're also becoming obsolete. James Abbington, in his book, *If It Had Not Been for the Lord on My Side* comments:

> In spite of the plethora of hymnbooks available today, the repertoire of hymns sung by main-line African American church congregations consists of fewer than fifty hymns, including Christmas carols and Easter hymns (Abbington, 138).

Moreover, church worship services feature music sung in unison, sometimes from a pre-recorded track. Music directors, all too often, choose worship music independently of the pastor or a music committee. Thus, it is not uncommon for pastors and music directors to disagree over what is acceptable worship music. The result is that many pastors, fearing that arguments with the music staff will cause

169

problems in the church, take the path of least resistance. Another area of concern is the inadequate preparation of pastors in the area of church music ministry. There are pastors who aren't musicians or who lack a musical background. Therefore, they aren't equipped to make informed decisions about sacred music selections. Too often, little emphasis is given to worship practices, liturgical traditions, and sacred music in seminaries.

The Sacred Duty of Church Music

Church music has a sacred duty, and pastors are charged with keeping the traditions of our musical heritage alive in the twenty-first century. Church leaders, regardless of their musical training, must acknowledge the connectedness between the preached and sung gospel. Wright gives this advice to pastors to remedy this situation: "A lot of preachers get threatened by the music. The music is essential. The music ushers in the spirit. It makes preaching easy. Stop fighting with the musicians. Work together as a team."

Obery Hendricks, in his treatise *The Universe Bends Toward Justice: Radical Reflections on the Bible, the Church, and the Body Politic* (2011) wrote a scathing indictment of gospel music. The first chapter of the book addresses the problems that plague gospel music in the twenty-first century. He views contemporary music as a deterrent to the social justice thesis of the Gospel of Jesus Christ:

> Gospel music has gained the world, but it has lost the prophetic heart of black sacred music, i.e., the biblical Exodus and its divine mandate of freedom... the ongoing social, political, and economic dilemmas that confront black people in America. At worst, gospel music today actually undermines collective social efforts—especially among African Americans—to address those dilemmas (4).

Black Sacred Music and the Pathos of Black People

Black sacred music, historically, has always addressed the pathos and struggles of black people in America. The spirituals were the first songs that collectively expressed the pathos of slavery and oppression. They contain the essence of what we define as black sacred music. They established the criteria of the genre. In the pre-gospel years, Charles Tindley wrote the words to the song that became a rallying cry during the Civil Rights Movement, "We Shall Overcome." Lucie Campbell, mentor to Thomas Dorsey, presented pageants that spoke to our history such as "Ethiopia at the Bar of Justice" and "Ethiopia, Stretch Forth Your Hand Unto God (Hendricks, 23)." Thomas Dorsey, continuing in that tradition, wrote songs to uplift the people during the Depression—to give them hope. He explained:

> I wrote to give [the people] something to lift them out of that depression…we intended Gospel to strike a happy medium for the downtrodden. This music lifted people out of the muck and mire of poverty and loneliness, of being broke, and gave them some kind of overall significance of hope (Hendricks, 16).

An Accountability to Address Moral Ills in Song

Two songs that Dorsey composed to comfort and edify God's people were "I've Got a Feeling" and "The Lord Will Make a Way Somehow." Dorsey also stressed his singers' accountability for addressing, through song, the moral ills of society (McLin Interview). However, an emphasis on the "good news" of gospel hindered them from addressing the ills of the society—the "bad news." Hendricks laments this fact:

[Gospel's] studied unwillingness to critique the bad news of the injustice and exploitation suffered by black folks, has contributed to the maintenance of the oppressive American social order by domesticating the outrage—that otherwise would have fueled political resistance and activism for the purpose of establishing a more just American society—into an emotion-laden apocalyptic hope (23).

Some of the greatest gospel songs composed and performed during the "Golden Age" of gospel did address the struggles of blacks in a racist society while celebrating the victories that were won. Among them are "How I Got Over "by Mahalia Jackson, "Any Day Now" by The Soul Stirrers, and the pageants "From Auction Block to Glory" and "Deep Dark Waters" produced by Herbert Brewster (Hendricks, 24).

Black Sacred Music as an Enterprise

Despite the intentional message of the spirituals, black sacred music has departed from its origins. No longer is it a collective outpouring of our hopes and anguish. It has evolved into a highly selective, individualized, and specialized enterprise that emphasizes performance more than social consciousness. It is entertainment, not social commentary, a commodity—a for-profit enterprise; consequently, it no longer belongs to the black church.

In Rev. Robert Earl Houston's article on the "Demise of Gospel Music," he writes that the gospel song has three functions: [to relate] "the powerful story of Jesus Christ, the powerful witness of God the Father, and the powerful abilities of the Holy Spirit." Houston praises music that "edifies, encourages, and reaches the soul," but he admonishes: "I pray that, just like we say "Keep Christ in Christmas," that we won't have to modify that mantra one day and say "Keep Christ in Gospel Music." However, I'm afraid that time is fast approaching (The Wire, 2014).

Hendricks takes a dimmer view, however, and questions whether gospel music today can even be considered black sacred music.

> As a genre, gospel music lacks most of the normative elements of sacred music that evolved through blacks' sojourn in America. Rather than collective acknowledgment of oppression, gospel offers individualized expressions of hope and praise. Instead of prophetic critique, it offers political quietism. Gospel songs do not exhort resistance to injustice; they counsel joyful resignation instead. Thus, we must conclude that other than its empathic dimension, gospel music today does not embody the normative features of black sacred music.... (34).

It is of vital importance that black sacred music continue as a genre. It is fundamental and integral to the religious worship experience of the Black Church. It is even more important that it address pressing concerns of the twenty-first century that threaten its survival. Black people have lived in America for about four hundred years, and still we are fighting for justice. Our children are being killed in the streets, both by each other and also by those who are sworn to protect them.

Churches are vacant, half-filled, or overflowing. Ministers and church leaders have a choice before them. They must decide between theology "God-talk" and "people speak." Will they preach the gospel, or entertain the congregation? What defines the African-American sacred religious experience in the twenty-first century? Do we preach about a God of liberation, or do we sing about escape to the heavenly world with no attempt to correct today's ills?

Praise and worship was originally defended as a way to involve the worshipper in the worship experience. The emphasis today has shifted from the choir, who traditionally led the congregation, to the congregant to make him or her a full participant in the worship experience. But a congregation's participation in praise and worship doesn't mean that God is being worshipped... Worship looks up to God—not to the latest dance moves. God is Spirit, and we must worship Him in spirit and in truth. That doesn't mean that we lose Christ and God in the process. We must know whom we are singing about and who is the focus of our praise, adoration, and joy.

The Lasting Contribution of Thomas A. Dorsey

We acknowledge with gratitude the contribution that Thomas A. Dorsey made to our musical heritage. We revere and value the tenacity that it took to bring music into the church that helped black people cope with the oppression and lack of opportunity that existed for them during the Depression years. We appreciate the many songs that he wrote to uplift, comfort, and edify the people of God. Appendix VI of this book features a selected list of the scores of sacred songs that he wrote. Countless musicians and singers have benefitted from his music and his legacy. Through his work, souls are continually encouraged and fed.

It is time, however, for twenty-first century musicians, singers, composers, and preachers to address the issues that black Americans still must confront in America. Let's continue to push for the equality and social justice that began our musical heritage from the Negro spirituals. Let us compose a new generation of songs to stir the hearts and consciousness of people to action. We are a people who express ourselves with our bodies in song and in dance. We can continue to praise God and begin to right some of the wrongs that continue in this "land of the free and home of the brave."

Music—sacred and secular—was a sustaining force in the life of our ancestors. Black music has always addressed concerns in the history of oppression that characterized life for people of African ancestry in The United States. Slavery and the civil rights era were the two major periods in time where this legacy was most evident. Black music, at that time, addressed civil rights issues in America as well as injustice throughout the world.

Marvin Gaye, the late secular singer from a Levitical heritage, composed a message of freedom and liberation in his masterpiece— "What's Going On"— a prophetic statement that addressed social issues of the 1960s. Its message—fifty years later—is relevant to the violence and killings that extend around the world. Music, sacred and secular, will always exist as a powerful tool that helps to shape and define the cultural landscape and mirror the injustices present in the society. Finally, it is important to remember that singing defines the Christian church (Ephesians 5:19). Singing, says Abbington:

> ...must be a purposeful act...it should be biblically based, theologically based, and relevant to the culture of the congregation. And most important, each member should depart the sanctuary worship vowed to say and mean, in the words of Thomas A. Dorsey, "I'm Going to Live the Life I Sing about in My Song," as the African American church continues to "Lift Every Voice and Sing!" remembering and affirming that, "If It Had Not Been for the Lord on My Side, Where Would I Be"?

The Columbian Exposition and World's Fair of 1893 attracted many blacks to Chicago. Southern blacks worked at, visited, or performed at the fair. Among them was Robert Abbott, who performed as a member of the Hampton Institute Quartet and migrated to Chicago in 1897. He founded the *Chicago Defender*, which became the nation's leading black newspaper in 1905. The paper was smuggled to southerners by black railroad porters and was circulated throughout the South, most notably in Mississippi. It enticed many southerners to leave for greater opportunities in Chicago and other places in the North and West.

Chicago, with its sizable black community, had numerous black businesses and civic organizations before World War I and became known as the "Promised Land" with job opportunities. Religious freedom existed to some degree in the northern colonies before the Civil War. The African American Church was firmly rooted after the Civil War and grew during the period known as "Reconstruction."

The Black Church as a Socializing Agent

The Black Church was the only available socializing agent for the newly arrived migrant. They established programs to educate the new arrivals on the customs and expectations of their newfound city life. Housing during that influx of blacks from the South was limited to a narrow strip of land south from the area known as Chicago's "Loop," an area that was cordoned off mostly by State Street on the west and Wentworth on the east.

Isabel Wilkerson wrote a masterful saga chronicling the migration of blacks from the South to the East, Midwest, and West. Her book, *The Warmth of Other Suns: The Epic Story of America's Great Migration (2011)* followed three individuals to Harlem, Chicago, and

176

Los Angeles. She describes the conditions that these three individuals faced, met, and lived with as a result of their decision to leave the South. It depicts the Jim Crow beliefs and practices of the white dominant sub-cultures that were structured to impede the economic and social progress of black emigrants.

Several events occurred in the North to provide social activities and to address civic problems, both nationally and locally. Sororities and fraternities were established. Civil rights organizations fought for the rights guaranteed by the amendments to the U.S. Constitution of the United States of America. The National Association for the Advancement of Colored People (NAACP) erupted from DuBois's advocacy in Buffalo's Niagara Movement of 1905. These efforts were devised to make inroads for Negroes into mainstream society.

Kalil compiled a roster of African American churches in Chicago during this period—churches whose members were instrumental in black religious, social, and civic affairs. Quinn Chapel A.M.E. stands out as the historical African Methodist Episcopal Church in Chicago. Its congregation served as a stop on the "Underground Railroad," using their homes as waystations during the Civil War. A table of those churches is found in Table 1 on the next page. The two landmark Baptist churches of Chicago's West Side—First Baptist Congregational and Metropolitan Missionary Baptist Church—had not been established under their present names in 1905 (Kalil 1993, 13-31). *The Colored People's Directory and Blue Book of Chicago, Illinois* (1905) lists the churches and businesses that existed for blacks who formed the first great wave of migrants to the city. Church conventions were organized. Newer denominations grew from the first established churches and conventions.

Table 1: African American Churches in Chicago during the 1900s

Name	Address	Pastor
Quinn Chapel AME	2401 S. Wabash Ave.	Rev. D. P. Roberts, M.D.
Bethel AME	30th and Dearborn Sts.	Rev. A.J. Carey, D.D.
Wayman Chapel AME	280 N. Franklin St.	Rev. J.C. Anderson, L.L.B
St. Stephens AME	682 Austin Ave.	Rev. W. S. Brooks D.D.
The Institutional Church and Social Settlement	3825 S. Dearborn	Revs. J.M. Townsend and D.D. Warden, Pastors
St. Mary AME	4926 S. Dearborn St.	Rev. J.P. Woods, A.B.; B.D., Pastor
St. John AME Church	63rd and Throop Sts.	Rev. James Higgins, Pastor
Hyde Park AME Church	5539 Jefferson St.	Rev. Andrew M. Webb, Pastor
Trinity AME Mission and Culture Center	155 18th St.	Rev. J.J. Wright, A.B.; B.D. Pastor
Allen Chapel AME Church	Avondale, IL	Rev. C.R. Doggin, Pastor
Walter's AMEZ Church	1086 W. Lake St	Rev. O.H. Banks, Pastor
Ebenezer Missionary Baptist Church	4857 S. Armour Ave.	Rev. J.F. Thomas, D.D., Pastor
Providence Baptist Church	26 N. Irving St.	Rev. A.L. Harris, B.D., Pastor
Olivet Baptist Church	27th and Dearborn Sts.	Rev. E.J. Fisher, D.D.; LLD, Pastor
St. John Baptist Church	2621 Armour Ave.	Rev. F.A. McCoo, D.D., Pastor

Friendship Baptist Church	Lake and Ann Sts.	Rev. H.W. Knight, Pastor
Hermon Baptist Church	757 N. Clark St.	Rev. Jordan Chavis, Pastor
Shiloh Baptist Church	Corner of May and 62nd Sts.	Rev. D.H. Harris D.D., Pastor
Berean Baptist Church	4838 Dearborn St.	Rev.W.S. Bradden, D.D., Pastor
Mt. Moriah Baptist Church	4332 State St.	Rev. J.B. Odom, Pastor
Central Union Baptist Church	3705 State St.	Rev. J.M. Mason D.D., Pastor
St. Paul Baptist Church	5540 Lake Ave.	Rev. W.R. Davis, Pastor
Butler Mission	224 W. 47th St.	Rev. William Gray, Pastor
Mt. Carmel Baptist Church	Oak Park, IL	Rev. E.F.D. Zimmerman, Pastor
Palestine Freewill Baptist Church	3751 Wood St.	Rev. J.T. King, Pastor
Primitive Baptist Church	3608 Armour Ave.	Rev. P.A. Bedford, Pastor
Bethesda Baptist Church	3232 State St.	Rev. George E. Duncan Sr. Pastor
South Side Christian Church of Christ	3329 State St.	M.T. Brown, Pastor

Christian Church Mission	3600 Armour	W.G. Kirk, Pastor
St. Monica Catholic Church	36th and Dearborn Sts.	Rev. D.J. Reardon, Temporary Pastor
St. Thomas Episcopal Church	30th St. near Dearborn	Rev. A.H. Lealted, Priest
St. Mark's M.E. Church	4752 Armour Ave.	Rev. W.H.Vaughn, Pastor
Scott Chapel M.E.	618 Fulton St.	Rev. D.H.V. Purnell, A.B. Pastor
Church of God Saints of Christ Tabernacle One	4721 Armour Ave.	Rev. E. Kennedy, Pastor
Grace Presbyterian Church	3409 Dearborn St.	Rev. Moses A. Jackson, Pastor
Hope Cumberland Presbyterian Church	6317 Carpenter St.	Rev Mr. Orton, Pastor
Old Time Methodist Church	3521 S. Dearborn St.	Rt.Rev. B.J. Brown, Pastor
Queen Esther Mission	5040 State St.	Mrs. Mary E. Lark Hill Pastor, Noted Evangelist and Black Prophetess
Mt. Zion Bethel Israel of God's Church	3203 State	Rev. G.W. Flowers, Pastor
White Horse Army	2842 La Salle St.	Rev. E. M. Pettis, Pastor

Note: Rev. H.H. White, former pastor of Olivet Baptist Church, General Baptist Missionary for the State of Illinois: Editor-in-Chief of the *American Review* and author of *The Church and the World* was also listed in the directory.
Source: Colored Peoples Directory of 1905:13-31

The "Black Metropolis"

This black migration was the catalyst for the vibrant black community known as "The Black Metropolis" that developed on Chicago's South

Side. This community was very similar to the "Black Wall Street" of Tulsa, Oklahoma, before it was destroyed by white rioters in the early years of the twentieth century.

Blacks were represented in various occupations. South siders in 1910 were employed in varied occupations, with the greatest being musicians, followed by physicians, actors, clergymen, teachers, lawyers, artists, showmen, and nurses (Drake, 121). Photographers, dentists, editors and reporters, chemists, civil engineers, architects, designers, and draftsmen concluded the occupations (Drake, 78).

Chicago's first African-American member of the U.S. House of Representatives, Oscar De Priest, was elected from the community in 1928. Black businesses catered to the needs of the residents. Commercial goods were produced by them for the community. Institutions grew from the perceived and concrete needs of the people. Jesse Binga established a bank for the people of the community.

The Supreme Life Insurance Company of America was chartered to provide for the needs of the community residents. Anthony Overton established The Overton Hygienic Company, the first Black cosmetic firm in Chicago (IIT Bronzeville Abstract). The *Chicago Defender*, first known as the *Black Dispatch*, was the voice of the people.

World War I ended European migration, and white males went to war. Labor companies went south to fill the labor shortage. The Illinois Central Railroad was asked by the mayor of New Orleans to stop carrying Negroes to the North, a request that was denied (Kalil, 29). Blacks, viewing Chicago as a desirable site, continued to arrive in large numbers during these three large migrations. Black migration patterns are illustrated in Table 2 shown below.

There are different dates and numbers provided for the migration of African-Americans from the South to the North, Midwest, and West. Most estimates agree that between five and six million people

181

were involved in these time periods. Migration occurred continuously after Recontructions for southern blacks. These time periods, however, are thought by experts to involve the greatest numbers of persons seeking a better life.

Table 2: Significant African-American Migration Patterns

Northern Migration	1840s-1890s
The Great Migration	1910s-1930s
The Second Migration	1940-1970s

A different trend has been seen since 1965. Northern blacks are reclaiming their southern heritage. Large numbers have left the urban cities of Chicago, Los Angeles, and New York. This reverse migration has accounted for an increase in the number of blacks who reside in the southern states. The reasons for blacks' returning to the South, paradoxically, are the same as those attributed to southern blacks who originally migrated to these cities. Plentiful jobs, better housing, lower costs of living, and genealogical ties are among the leading factors responsible for these demographic changes.

Jim Crow Moves North

Blacks had hoped that they had left Jim Crow, segregation, and lynching behind in the South. Newly arrived southern immigrants found instead that they had replaced cotton boundaries with those of steel and concrete. There were no visible colored or white signs to mark territory and designate first and second class citizenship, but the hatred and unrelenting oppression remained the same. Contact with other ethnicities occurred only at work. Other forms of contact took the shape of riots and destruction of black property.

Arriving blacks were able to acquire only the lowest paying jobs, those that no one else wanted. This was the pattern of twentieth century America, and, sadly, is seen far too often in the twenty-first century as well. Newly arrived blacks found employment only as porters and domestic workers. They were forced to take unhealthy jobs in steel mills and packinghouses with no chance for promotion—regardless of their ability. Trade unions instituted "grandfather" status that blocked blacks from entry into employment in those fields.

Chicago's Racial Divide: 1919-1930

Tensions continued to grow over restrictions in union contracts that excluded blacks, the lack of decent wages, and overcrowding in the "Black Belt." White landowners continued the practice of sub-dividing living spaces to force more and more people to live in substandard conditions. Neighborhoods in Chicago became the visible markers of segregation. Property owners made certain streets dividing lines for incoming blacks. They signified the composition of the residents by color.

Each successive wave of migration from the South intensified and fueled bigotry and racism, forcing black migrants into inadequate housing facilities. Landowners rushed to make huge profits from cutting up larger apartments into rooms with a shared kitchen and bathroom. Most of these housing rooms were called "kitchenettes." These injustices fueled anger and resentment by blacks toward whites in the city.

Tensions flared over housing and the enrollment of Negroes in public schools. There were open race wars. Blacks had been denied educational opportunities in the South beyond mostly one-room schoolhouses. Their enrollments now in well-equipped and modern northern schools resulted only because of compulsory education laws. Night school was another option for educational advancement. Most blacks found out, however, after graduation, that they were still denied entry into the labor force except in the lowest paying and dirtiest jobs.

The Emergence of Bronzeville

The end of World War 1 brought some changes in the housing patterns and lifestyles of African- Americans in Chicago. Racial segregation was still rigidly enforced, but the Black Belt had continued to move into formerly all-white territories. The black population had grown steadily from 1910 to 1920. Middle class blacks began moving into formerly white neighborhoods.   Bronzeville was one such community that resulted from those inroads.

The area that became known as Bronzeville included three black Chicago neighborhoods on the south side of Chicago. These neighborhoods have the official names of Douglas, Grand Boulevard, and Kenwood. They were the "heart and soul" of the south side black community. The liner notes from a Paramount Records record album of the time described the history of this collective black community known as Bronzeville (IIT: HEALD Archives—Bronzeville Collection 2001-2005).

The blues composition titled "Lovin's Been Here and Gone to Mecca Flats," by Jimmie Blythe shared a story of lost love in this housing complex. The origin of the title "Mecca Flats" was derived from a building erected in 1892 located on 34th Street between State and Dearborn. It was a four-story horseshoe-shaped building with an exterior courtyard, two interior glass-covered atria, and 650 apartments. These apartments were originally designed for the city's middle class white residents (IIT Bronzeville abstract). Its previous use had been as temporary quarters for visitors to the 1893 World's Columbian Exposition.

This usage changed drastically after the first migration from the South brought thousands of new Black residents to Chicago in

184

less than a decade. Bruck writes that "Black businessmen and women, professionals, and middle-class families settled into The Mecca as Chicago's wealthy white residents left the South Side for the North Shore" (IIT Bronzeville Abstract). The real estate companies partitioned single family homes originally built in the 1890s as mansions for wealthy white Chicagoans into multiple apartments for black occupancy.

The Chicago Riot of 1919

The return of white soldiers to their homes following World War 1 contributed to the increased racial tensions. Klu Klux Klansmen throughout the country were involved in open acts of terror. The summer of 1919 became known as "Red Summer" throughout the nation as one after another reports of violence and killings were reported. One explanation given by the media for these acts of aggressions by whites toward blacks involved the lack of work and housing for the returned soldiers.

One bloody riot testifying to this hatred and racism occurred in Chicago on July 27, 1919, a year after Thomas Dorsey arrived in Chicago. A black youth was stoned until he drowned for crossing the invisible line that separated the black and white swimming rights on Lake Michigan's south side beach around 29th Street. Recreational facilities, parks and beaches, were strictly segregated (Khalil, 35). The police did nothing to the white man witnesses identified as causing the attack by a group of white boys.

Ensuing riots lasted many days during which both black and white groups attacked anyone caught in the wrong part of town at any time. The governor's request for intervention of the National Guard didn't come in enough time (they didn't arrive until July 30, 1919) to prevent the bloodshed that occurred. By then, many blacks were left homeless. Twenty-three blacks and fifteen whites were dead. Five-hundred thirty seven people were injured. Property damage exceeded one million dollars (Aguiar, 1999).

After this riot, the Chicago Commission on Race Relations was formed. Chicagoans offered up many suggestions to prevent future violent occurrences ranging from legalized segregation through zoning ordinances to work-enforced restrictions in industries. Liberal whites and blacks alike rejected these alternatives.

The End of "Mecca Flats"

The history of subsequent riots in America, however, replicate the racial truths of 1919. The findings of the Kerner Commission almost fifty years later underscored the lack of movement toward the premise that "all men are created equal" of our Constitution. The report concluded that "The United States of America was moving toward two societies, one black, and one white— separate and unequal." Unless conditions were remedied, the Commission warned, the country faced a "system of apartheid" in its major cities (The Kerner Report, 1967, The National Advisory Commission on Civil Disorder).

The problem of the black presence after that summer was addressed by city "eminent domain" laws and an expansion of colleges and universities. The commercial center of Bronzeville had shifted east and south to Prairie and South Park (later renamed Dr. Martin Luther King, Drive. The neighborhood, however, managed to remain vibrant through the 1950s. "Bronzeville residents" writes Bruck, "continued to welcome relatives, friends and new families into the area (Bruck, 2014)."

Extended family members and boarders who could help pay the rent came to share the apartments. Thus, the Mecca became increasingly overcrowded, over-used and under stress. Subsequently, the Illinois Institute of Technology acquired the land and demolished Mecca Flats. "The last of the Mecca residents moved out in 1951, and the once grand nineteenth century building was razed to make way for Ludwig Mies van der Rohe's S.R. Crown Hall (Bruck, 2014)." One of the few existing landmarks of the era, Thomas Dorsey's home church, Pilgrim Baptist Church, remains to this day in the historic community of Bronzeville.

Core Dimension

The core dimension "valued reality"of this three dimensional model relates to how the individual moves in interaction with self and others. Patterns of interaction develop as a person moves and grows in relation to her or his conceptualization of self as subject (intuitively, internally) [subjective reality] and self as object (consensually, externally) [objective reality]. This awareness gradually merges in the person and becomes her or his personal reality map."

Appendix III:

Timeline of the Development of the National Convention of Gospel Choirs and Choruses 1933-2014	
New Orleans, LA - 81st Session	2014
	2013
Houston, TX - 80th Session	
	2012
Washington, D.C. - 79th Session Dr. Marabeth Gentry installed as first female NCGCC President.	
	2011
Atlanta, GA - 78th Session Convention commemorates the passing of our beloved President, Bishop Kenneth H. Moales, Sr.	
Orlando, FL - 77th Session. Death of NCGCC President Bishop Kenneth H. Moales, Sr. Convention commemorates the passing of Min. Ted Thomas and Chairman Emeritus George "Buddy" Davis	2010
Las Vegas, NV - 76th Session	2009
Chicago, IL - 75th Anniversary	2008
Louisville, KY - 74th Session	2007
St. Louis, MO - 73rd Session Death of Dr. Bruce Warren	2006
Orlando, FL - 72nd Session	2005
Buffalo, NY - 71st Session	2004
Washington, DC - 70th Session	2003
Nashville, TN - 69th Session	2002
Houston, TX - 68th Session	2001
New Orleans, LA - 67th Session George "Buddy" Davis, new Chairman of the Board	2000
Orlando, FL - 66th Session	1999

Charlotte, NC - 65th Session	1998
Atlanta, GA - 64th Session	1997
Baltimore, MD - 63rd Session	1996
Cleveland, OH - 62nd Session	1995
Cincinnati, OH - 61st Session	1994
Death of Willa Mae Ford Smith	
Chicago, IL - 60th Session	1993
Death of Dr. Thomas A. Dorsey, NCGCC Founder and President	
Rev. Kenneth Moales named president	1992
Winston-Salem, NC - 59th Session	1991
Miami, FL - 58th Session	
Birmingham, AL - 57th Session	1990
Death of Joshua Gentry	
Rev. Kenneth Moales appointed interim President	1989
Toledo, OH - 56th Session	1988
Washington, DC - 55th Session	1987
Nashville, TN - 54th Session	
Louisville, KY - 53rd Session	1986
Philadelphia, PA - 52nd Session	1985
Buffalo, NY - 51st Session	1984
Chicago, IL - 50th Session	1983
Orlando, FL - 49th Session	1982
Due to ill health of Dr. Dorsey, Joshua Gentry assumes presidential duties.	
"Say Amen, Somebody" recorded	
Houston, TX - 48th Session	1981
New York, NY - 47th Session	1980
Louisville, KY - 46th Session	1979

Atlanta, GA - 45th Anniversary	1978
Pittsburgh, PA - 44th Session	1977
Chicago, IL - 43rd Session Death of Fannie Foster Geneva Gentry appointed to head Consecration Service	1976
Cleveland, TN - 42nd Session	1975
St. Louis, MO - 41st Session	1974
Cincinnati, OH - 40th Session	1973
Washington, D.C. - 39th Session First convention to be held in a hotel	1972
Los Angeles, CA - 38th Session Home for singers purchased and built in Chicago	1971
Detroit, MI - 37th Session	1970
Philadelphia, PA - 36th Session	1969
Louisville, KY - 35th Session	1968
Houston, TX - 34th Session Alumni Chorale founded by Rev. Earl Preston Registration opens in the parent body	1967
Buffalo, NY - 33rd Session	1966
Chicago, IL - 32nd Session	1965
Huntington, WV - 31st Session	1964
Pittsburgh, PA - 30th Session	1963
St. Louis, MO - 29th Session	1962
Philadelphia, PA - 28th Session	1961
Washington, D.C. - 27th Session	1960
Philadelphia, PA - 26th Session First known Gospel musical drama	1959

Chicago, IL - 25th Session   1958

Louisville, KY - 24th Session   1957

Detroit, MI - 23rd Session   1956
James Cleveland Youth Dept. Music Director along
with the O'Neal Twins

Buffalo, NY - 22nd Session   1955

21st Session.   1954
Youth registration begins

Memphis, TN - 20th Session   1953

Minneapolis, MN - 19th Session   1952

OH - 18th Session.   1951

Cincinnati, OH - 17th Session   1950
Leadership Training School founded by Artelia Hutchins

Huntington, WV - 16th Session   1949
Death of Magnolia Butts
Fannie Foster appointed over Consecration Service

15th Session   1948

14th Session   1947
(Soloist Bureau features Mahalia Jackson,
Delois Barrett, O'Neal Twins, Joe Mays,
and Geneva Gentry

Chicago, IL - 13th Session   1946

Detroit, MI - 12th Session   1945
Purchased building for school in Chicago.

Huntington, WV - 11th Session   1944
Soloist Council name changed to Soloist Bureau

Cincinnati, OH - 10th Session	1943
St. Louis, MO - 9th Session	1942
Joshua Gentry Youth President with youth members	
Della Reese, Dinah Washington, and Aretha Franklin	
New York, NY - 8th Session	1941
Chicago, IL - 7th Session	1940
E. St. Louis, IL - 6th Session	1939
Junior Department (Youth Dept.) founded by Dr. Theodore Frye,	
with Ruth Hutchins, President, Joshua Gentry First Vice-President,	
Roberta Martin, First Junior Dept. Supervisor	
Soloist Council founded by Willa Mae Ford Smith	
Dayton, OH - 5th Session	1938
Consecration Service instituted by Magnolia Butts	
Indianapolis, IN - 4th Session	1937
Vesper service started and led by Dr. Theodore Frye	
Detroit, MI - 3rd Session	1936
Founders' Day instituted; Artist Night instituted by Magnolia Butts	
Cincinnati, OH - 2nd Session	1935
Scholarship Department founded by Magnolia Butts	
St. Louis, MO - 1st Session	1934
Dorsey Day instituted	
Advisory Board adopted	
Chicago, IL – First bylaws adopted	1933
Dr. Thomas A. Dorsey elected president	

* Sources: NCGCC Website 2nd Vice President Dr. Bessie M. Palmer

APPENDIX IV: PERIODS OF BLACK SACRED MUSIC DEVELOPMENT

1619 - 1800	Beginning of slave musical expressions
1760 - 1875	Creation of the Negro Spiritual
1800 - 1900	Meter music of Watts; Great Awakening
1875 - 1925	Euro hymns with black rhythm
1925 - 1940	Classical Gospel Era
1945 - 1970	Golden/Modern Gospel Era
1968 - 1990	Crossover Gospel Era
1990 - Present	Contemporary Gospel Era

Adapted from Walker, 1979, *Somebody's Calling My Name*

Appendix V: Development of Gospel Music 1900-2015

Pre-gospel
1900-1920

1900
Hymnody
Evangelism
Quartets
Blues and Jazz

1910
Black and white
Hymnody
Lucie Campbell
Charles Tindley

Developmental 1920s-1940s
Thomas Dorsey, "Father of Gospel Music" and Dorsey's "Disciples" (1920)
1930 NCGCC founded by Dorsey, Martin, and Frye (1930)
Alex Bradford Singers; Alex Bradford, composer
Chicago: Gospel Mecca

Golden Age 1940s-1960s
Community Gospel Choirs—Thompson Community Singers (1940)
Wooten Chorale Ensemble Southside Community Choir
Female singing groups: Davis Sisters, Ward Sisters, Sallie Martin Singers Roberta Martin Singers
Quartets, The Caravans, Original Gospel Harmonettes, The Williams Brothers
Solo vocal styles—Sister Rosetta Tharpe

1950 Gospel Highway
Expansion of gospel music publishing, radio, and recording
Gospel industry outside the church
Crossover of gospel singers to secular music
Refinement of traditional gospel choir sound

Contemporary: 1960s-2015
1960s—Influence of secular music increases
James Cleveland founds GMWA
Gospel choirs record throughout the nation
Andrae Crouch, Walter Hawkins, Jessy Dixon Singers
Edwin Hawkins: Father of Contemporary Gospel

195

1970s New Era
Winans Family, The Clark Sisters, Rance Allen Group
Staples Singers

1980s Expansion: Redefinition of Gospel Music
Richard Smallwood Singers, Vanessa Bell Armstrong
Hezekiah Walker/Love Fellowship, Dottie Peoples

1990s Urban influence
Kirk Franklin and New Nation, Kurt Karr Singers,
Donnie McClurkin Israel Houghton
Donald Lawrence and Tri-City Singers
Yolanda Adams, Ricky Dillard and New Generation

2000s New Millennium Urban Contemporary Gospel
Tye Tribbett, Kim Burrell, Tamela Mann
Mary Mary, Ernest Pugh, Tonex
Smokie Norful, Marvin Sapp, James Fortune and FIYA

2000-Present Urban Contemporary Gospel
J. Moss
Charles Jenkins and Fellowship Chicago
William McDowell
Tasha Cobbs
VaShawn Mitchell

Adapted from Wise (2002)

Appendix VI:
Selected List of Sacred Songs by Thomas A. Dorsey

A

"A Crown for Me"

"All Alone"

"An Angel Spoke to Me Last Night"

"Angels Keep Watching Over Me"

B

"Be Thou Near Me All the Way"

"Beautiful Tomorrow"

"Behold the Man of Galilee"

C

"Changes"

"Come Unto Me"

"Come Ye That Love the Lord"

"Consideration"

"Count Your Blessings from the Lord Each Day"

D

"Diamonds from the Crown of the Lord"

"Did It Happen to You Like It Happened to Me?"

"Did You Ever Say to Yourself, 'I Love Jesus'?"

"Does Anybody Here Know My Jesus?"

"Does It Mean Anything to You?"

"Don't Forget the Name of the Lord"

"Don't You Need My Savior, Too?"

"Down by the Side of the River"

E

"Ev'ry Day Will Be Sunday By and By"

F

"Forgive Me Lord, and Try Me One More Time"

"Forgive My Sins, Forget, and Make Me Whole"

G

"Get Ready and Serve the Lord"

"Give Me a Voice to Sing Thy Praise"

"Glory for Me"

"God Be with You"

"Gospel Medley"

H

"He Brought Me All the Way"

"He Has Gone to Prepare a Place for Me"

"He Is Risen, for He's Living in My Soul"

"He Is the Same Today"

"He Never Will Leave Me"

"He'll Know Me over Yonder"

"He's All I Need"

"He's the Joy of My Salvation"

"Hide Me in Thy Bosom"

"Hold Me (Please Don't Let Me Go)"

"Hold on a Little While Longer"

"How about You?"

"How Many Times"

"How Much More of Life's Burden Can We Bear?"

I

"I am a Pilgrim, I Am a Stranger"

"I Am His, and He Is Mine"

"I Can Depend on Jesus; He Can Depend on Me"

"I Can't Forget It, Can You?"

"I Claim Jesus First, and That's Enough for Me"

"I Don't Know What I'd Do Without Jesus"

"I Don't Know What I'd Do Without the Lord"

"I Don't Know What You Think of Jesus"

"I Don't Know Why I Have to Cry Sometime"

"I Got Heaven in My View"

"If You See My Savior"

"I Got Jesus in My Soul"

"I Have a Home"

"I Know It Was the Blood"

"I Know My Redeemer Lives"

"I May Never Pass This Way Again"

"I Thank God for My Song"

"I Thought on My Way"

"I Want Jesus on the Road I Travel"

"I Want to Be More Like Jesus"

"I Want to Go There"

"I Want Two Wings to Veil My Face"

"I'll Be Waiting for You at the Beautiful Gate"

"I'll Never Turn Back"

"I'll Take Jesus for Mine"

"I'm a Stranger; Don't Drive Me Away"

"I'm Climbing Up the Rough Side of the Mountain"

"I'm Goin' to Live the Life I Sing About in My Song"

"I'm Going to Follow Jesus All the Way"

"I'm Going to Wait Until My Change Shall Come"

"I'm Going to Walk Right in and Make Myself at Home"

"I'm in Your Care"

"I'm Just a Sinner Saved by Grace"

"I'm Satisfied with Jesus in My Heart"

"I'm Singing Everyday"

"I'm Talking about Jesus"

"I'm Waiting for Jesus; He's Waiting for Me"

"If You Ring the Bell"

"If We Never Needed the Lord Before, We Sure Do Need Him Now"

"If You Meet God in the Morning"

"If You Ring the Bell"

"If You Sing a Gospel Song"

"In the Scheme of Things"

"It Is Real with Me"

"It Is Thy Servant's Prayer A-men"

"It Just Suits Me"

"It's a Highway to Heaven"

"It's All in the Plan of Salvation"
"It's Jesus with You"
"It's Not a Shame to Cry Holy to the Lord"

J

"Jesus Is the Light"
"Jesus Never Does a Thing That's Wrong"
"Jesus Only"
"Jesus Remembers When Others Forget"
"Jesus Rose Again"
"Jesus, My Comforter"
"Just a Little While"
"Just One Step"

K

"Keep Me Everyday"

L

"Lead Me to the Rock That's Higher Than I"
"Let Me Understand"
"Let the Savior Bless Your Soul Right Now"
"Let Us Go Back to God"
"Let Us Pray Together"
"Life Can Be Beautiful"
"Look on the Brighter Side"
"Look Up"
"Lord, Look Down on Me"

M

"Make Me Pray"
"Make Me the Servant I Would Like to Be"
"Maybe It's You, and Then It's Me"
"Meet Me at the Pearly Gates"
"My Desire"
"My Faith I Place in Thee"

200

"My Mind on Jesus"
"My Soul Feels Better Right Now"
"My Soul Shall Live with Jesus"
"My Time's Not As Long As It Has Been"

N
"Never Leave Me Alone"

O
"O Lord Show Me the Way"
"O Who's Goin to Lead Me?"
"Old Ship of Zion"
"Old Time Spirituals"
"Our Father Who Art in Heaven: The Lord's Prayer"

P
"Precious Lord, Take My Hand: Take My Hand Precious Lord"

R
"Remember Me"
"Right Now"

S
"Save Me As I Am"
"The Savior Is Born"
"The Savior's Here"
"Say a Little Prayer for Me"
"Search Me Lord"
"Shake My Mother's Hand for Me"
"Sing in My Soul"
"Singing Everywhere"
"Singing My Way to Rest"
"Singing Tonight"

"Sleep on Mother"

"Somebody's Knocking at Your Door"

"Someday"

"Someday I'll Be at Rest"

"Someday I'm Going Home"

"Someday I'm Goin' to See My Lord"

"Someday, Somewhere"

"Something Has Happened to Me"

"Songbook—Songs of the Kingdom"

"Songbook—Songs with a Message"

"Standing Here Wondering Which Way to Go"

"Surely My Jesus Must Be True"

T

"Take Me Through, Lord"

"Tell Jesus Everything"

"Thank You All the Days of My Life"

"That's All That I Can Do"

"That's Good News"

"The Day Is Past and Gone"

"The Flag for You and Me: Patriotic Song"

"The Little Town Where I First Found the Lord: True to Life Song"

"The Lord Is My Shepherd"

"The Lord Knows Just What I Need"

"The Lord Will Make a Way Somehow"

"There Is Something about the Lord Mighty Sweet"

"There Isn't But One Way to Make It In"

"There'll Be Peace in the Valley for Me"

"There's a Better Day Coming Right Here"

"There's a God Somewhere"

"There's an Empty Chair at the Table"

"This Man Jesus"

"Thy Kingdom Come"

"Today (Evening Song)"

"Traveling On"

"Treasures in Heaven"

"Troubled about My Soul"

U

"Use My Heart, Use My Mind, Use My Hands"

W

"Walk Close to Me, Lord"

"Want to Go to Heaven When I Die"

"Wasn't That an Awful Time?"

"We Must Work Together"

"What Could I Do If It Wasn't for the Lord?"

"What the Good Lord's Done for Me"

"What the World Needs Is Jesus Most of All"

"What Then?"

"When Day Is Done"

"When I Can Read My Title Clear"

"When I've Done My Best"

"When I've Sung My Last Song"

"When the Gates Swing Open, Let Me In"

"When the Last Mile Is Finished"

"When They Crown Him Lord of All"

"When You Bow in the Evening at the Altar"

"While He's Passing By"

"Who Is Willing to Take a Stand for the Lord?"

"Windows of Heaven"

"Wings over Jordan"

"Won't You Come and Go Along?"

Y

"You Can't Go through This World by Yourself"

"Your Sins Will Find You Out"

Sheet Music included in the Dorsey Archives at Fisk University.

Abbington, James ed. *Readings in African American Church Music and Worship, Volume 1*. Chicago: GIA Publications, 2001.

Abbington, James, ed., *Readings in African American Church Music and Worship: Volume 2*. Chicago: GIA Publications, 2014.

Aguiar, Marian. "Chicago Riots of 1919," Microsoft Encarta Africana. Microsoft Corporation, 1999.

Baldwin, Davarian L. *Chicago's New Negroes: Modernity, The Great Migration and Black Urban Life*. Chapel Hill: The University of North Carolina Press, 2007.

Baldwin, Lewis V. *Plenty Good Room: A Bible Study based on African American Spiritual*. Nashville: Abingdon Press, 2002.

Best, Wallace D. *Passionately Human, No Less Divine Religion and Culture in Black Chicago 1915-1952*. Princeton: Princeton University Press, 2005.

Bethea, D.A., compiler. *Colored Peoples Blue Book and Business Directory of Chicago*. Chicago: Celerity Publishing Co., 1905.

Boschman, Lamar. *The Rebirth of Music*. Little Rock, AR: Manasseh Books, 2000.

Boyer, Horace C. *The Golden Age of Gospel*. Chicago: University of Illinois Press, 1995, 2000.

Bradley, D. H. *A History of the A.M.E. Zion Church*. New York: Columbia University Press, *(1956)*.

Broughton, Viv, *Black Gospel: An Illustrated History of the Gospel Sound*. Dorset, UK: Blandford Press, 1985.

Bruck, Catherine Archivist – 2002. *Bronzeville Collection – Abstract:* Chicago: IIT: Heald Archives 2001-2005.

Carpenter, Bill. *Uncloudy Days: The Gospel Music Encyclopedia*. San Francisco: Backbeat Books, 2005.

Carter, Janelle, "Rocking the Flock: More Churches Using Professional Musicians," *Dayton Daily News*, 4 September, 1999.

Chicago Commission on Race Relations. *The Negro in Chicago: A Study of Race Relations and a Riot*. Chicago: The University of Chicago Press, 1922.
(Chicago Defender. Monday, 30 Aug 1982, 16).

(Chicago Tribune. 1/24/93 Sec. 2

Darden, Robert. *People Get Ready.* New York: Continuum, 70-72, 2008.

Darden, Robert. *Nothing but Love in God's Water: Black Sacred Music from the Civil War to the Civil Rights Movement.* University Park, PA: Pennsylvania State University Press, 2014.

Demilinget, Sandor and John Steiner. *Destination Chicago Jazz.* Thomas Dorsey prepares his choir for a national television show in the early 1960s. Chicago: Arcadia Publishing, 36, 2003.

Dictionary of Christianity in America. Daniel G. Reid, Robert D. Linder, Bruce L. Shelley and Harry S. Stout, eds. Westmont, IL: InterVarsity Christian Fellowship/USA, 1990.

Dorsey, Thomas A., ed. Kenneth Morris, "Ministry of Music in the Church," *Improving the Music in the Church.* Chicago: Martin and Morris, 42, 1949.

Dorsey, Thomas A., *A Poem Book for All Occasions.* Chicago: 1945.

Dorsey, Thomas, Julia Smith and Mary White eds. *Songs with A Message No. 1.* Chicago: Thomas A. Dorsey, Publisher, 1951.

Dorsey, Thomas, Kathryn Dorsey and Julia Smith, eds. *Songs of Kingdom.* Chicago: Dorsey Publishing Company, 1954.

Drake, St. Clair. *Churches and Voluntary Associations in the Chicago Negro Community.* Chicago: Works Progress Administration, 1940.

Easton's Bible Dictionary, PC Study Bible formatted electronic database. Copyright © 2003, 2006 Biblesoft, Inc. All rights reserved.

Evanzz, Karl. *The Messenger: The Rise and Fall of Elijah Muhammad.* New York: Pantheon, 1999.

Felder, Cain Hope, ed. *Stony the Road We Trod: African American Biblical Interpretation.* Minneapolis: Fortress Press, 1991.

Franklin Aretha. *Aretha: From These Roots.* New York: Villard, 1999.

Gospelrama News, Vol.3, No. 9, Washington, DC, September 1982.
Heilbut, Anthony. *The Gospel Sound,* rev. ed. New York: Limelight, 1997.

Hendricks, Obery, M. Jr. *The Universe Bends Toward Justice: Radical Reflections on the*

Bible, the Church, and the Body Politic. Maryknoll, NY: Orbis Books, Kindle Edition, 2011.

Jackson, Jerma A. *Singing in My Soul: Black Gospel Music in a Secular Age.* Chapel Hill: The University of North Carolina Press, 2004.

Jackson, Jerma. *Testifying at the Cross: Thomas Andrew Dorsey, Sister Rosetta Tharpe and the Politics of African American Sacred and Secular Music.* Ann Arbor: UMI, 1995.

Jackson, L. "Choirs at Pilgrim (Pilgrim Baptist)." Federal Writers Project Negro Studies Project. New York: The New Press, 2003.

Kalil, Timothy Michael. "The Role of the Great Migration of African Americans to Chicago in the Development of traditional Black Gospel Piano by Thomas Dorsey." Ph.D. diss., UMI, 1993.

Kemp, Kathryn. *A Knowledge Theory Applied to Objective/Subjective Change through a Counselor Education Program.* Ed.D. diss.,UMI, 1983.

Kemp, Kathryn. *Make A Joyful Noise: A Brief History of Gospel Music Ministry in America.* Chicago: Joyful Noise Press, 20.

The Kerner Report, 1967. Report of The National Advisory Commission on Civil Disorder. www.eisenhowerfoundation.org

Lieb, Sandra. *Mother of the Blues—A Study of Ma Rainey.* Amherst, MA: University of Massachusetts Press, 1981.

Light, Alan "Say Amen, Somebody." *Vibe,* October 1997, 92-38.

Lovelace, Austin and William Rice. *Music and Worship in the Church. Nashville:* Abingdon Press, 1976.

McClain, William, Chairman of the National Advisory Task Force. *Songs of Zion Supplemental Worships Resources 12.* Nashville: Abingdon, 1981.

McWhirter, Cameron. "Red Summer: The Summer of 1919 and the Awakening of Black America." Chicago Tribune, 18 November 2011.

Muwakkil, Salim. *The Reader,* Vol 1, 28.30: 27 October 1978.

Peterson, Eugene H. *THE MESSAGE: The Bible in Contemporary Language,* Carol Stream, IL: NAVPress 2002.

Pratt, Waldo. *The History of Music.* New York: Selden G. Schirmer, 1907.

The Precious Lord Story and Gospel Songs by Thomas A. Dorsey. Bloomington, IN: Indiana School of Music Library, 1994.

Reagon, Bernice Johnson. *If You Don't Go Don't Hinder Me: The African American Sacred Song Tradition,* from the Abraham Lincoln Lecture Series. Lincoln: University of Nebraska Press, 2001.

Reagon, Bernice. *We'll Understand It Better By and By: Pioneering African American Gospel Composers.* Washington: Smithsonian Institution, 1992.

"The Real Thomas Dorsey." *Voice,* 5 October 1982, 94.

Reed, Teresa L. *The Holy Profane Religion in Black Popular Music.* Lexington, KY: The University Press of Kentucky, 2003.

Reich, Howard. *Chicago Tribune,* 24 January, 1993, Sec. 2, 1, 6.

Smith, Ruth. *The Life and Works of Thomas Andrew Dorsey, the Celebrated Pianist, Songwriter Poetical and Pictorial, Thomas A. Dorsey.* Chicago: Dorsey, 1935.

Smith, Theophus. *Conjuring Culture: Biblical Formations of Black America.* New York: Oxford: University Press, 1994.

Sollors, Werner, cf. *Beyond Ethnicity: Consent and Descent in American Culture.* New York: Oxford University Press, 1986.

Southern, Eileen. *The Music of Black Americans.* New York: W.W. Norton, 1971.

Tillotson, Edith. *Gospel Born: A Pictorial and Poetic History of the National Convention of Gospel Choirs and Choruses.* NCGCC, 1976.

Turner, Steve. *Early Spirituals to Contemporary Urban.* Oxford, England: Lion Hudson, 2010.

Walker, Wyatt Tee. *Somebody's Calling My Name: Black Sacred Music and Social Change.* Valley Forge, PA: Judson Press, 1979.

Walker, Wyatt Tee. James Abbington, ed. *Spirits That Dwell in Deep Woods: The Prayer and Praise Hymns of the Black Religious Experience.* Chicago: GIA Publications, Inc. 1991.

Willliams, Adina. "A Czech in the Land of Spirituals." *American Legacy: Special Music Edition Summer* 2009.
Wilmore, G. S. *Black Religion and Black Radicalism;*
An Interpretation of the Religious History of Afro-American People, Maryknoll,NY:

Orbis Books, 1983.

Wise, Raymond. "Defining African American Music by Tracing Its Historical and Musical Development from 1900-2000," Dissertation Project. Columbus, OH: Ohio State University; Wise, 2002.

Audio Recordings
Paramount Records 1927 phonograph "Lovin's Been Here and Gone to Mecca Flats" by Jimmie Blythe. The New York Laboratories, Port Washington, WI. Trademark Registered.

"Come on Mama, Do That Dance 1928-32." Georgia Tom Dorsey (Artist) Format: Audio CD Yazoo, 1041.

Georgia Tom (Thomas A. Dorsey Complete Recorded Works in Chronological Order Vol. 1: September 1928-5 February 1930. RST Records Blues Documents compiled and produced by Johnny Parth for RST Records Schonbrunner StraBe14, A-1050 Vienna, Austria.

"Say Amen Somebody," sound recording: original soundtrack recording and more, a George T. Nierenberg film: produced and mixed by Fordin, Hugh, New York DRG Records, 1983.

"Tampa Red, the Guitar Wizard." CD Columbia1994 Sony Entertainment, Inc., Sony Music Entertainment Inc. / Manufactured by Columbia Records NY. "Columbia Legacy" "Roots and Blues.

Hyperlinks
http://masonseminaryitc.org/
http://www.thebarcc.org/history.php
http://www.encyclopedia.chicagohistory.org/pages/929.html
http://civilwaybluegrass.net
http://hellobeautiful.com 2/9/14
http://issuu.com/cofield911/docs/august__cofield_report
https://www.pbs.org/thisfarbyfaith/transcript/episode_3.pdf
http://www.cityofchicago.org/dam/city/depts/zlup/Historic_Preservation/Publications/Black_Metropolis_Bronzeville.PDF

Index

210